THE KILLER'S BRAND

Dace Kelly is released from prison on the condition that he helps the warden's sister save her ranch outside Tolerance, Colorado. He and the Professor, who is also being released, ride there together. But Dace faces problems aplenty: the warden's sister doesn't want Dace there, a gunman is after him and a powerful rancher is after the lady's ranch. Then there's someone intent on seeing the Professor dead . . . Maybe Dace would have been a whole lot safer staying in prison!

TERRELL L. BOWERS

THE KILLER'S BRAND

Complete and Unabridged

LINFORD
Leicester

First published in Great Britain in 2008 by
Robert Hale Limited
London

First Linford Edition
published 2009
by arrangement with
Robert Hale Limited
London

British Library CIP Data

Bowers, Terrell L.
   The killer's brand - - (Linford western library)
   1. Western stories.
   2. Large type books.
   I. Title II. Series
   813.5′4–dc22

ISBN 978–1–84782–772–2

Published by
F. A. Thorpe (Publishing)
Anstey, Leicestershire

Set by Words & Graphics Ltd.
Anstey, Leicestershire
Printed and bound in Great Britain by
T. J. International Ltd., Padstow, Cornwall

This book is printed on acid-free paper

1

Three years of confinement at the Canyon City prison had taken its toll on Dace Kelly. Meals were a steady ration of beans, bread and water, with only an occasional onion or citrus to prevent scurvy. The physical work to help build a wall around the prison, combined with little rest from a few unfriendly prisoners or the watchful eye of the guards and he had grown as lean and haggard as a half-starved timber wolf.

'It's a big day for me,' Bernard said cheerfully, walking at his side. 'A final trip to the warden's office and then it is fresh air and freedom for the rest of my life.'

'Yep.'

'I know you still have five more years to languish in confinement, but what's the first thing you're going to do when you get out?' Bernard asked. 'Me . . . I'm going to find the nearest tavern or saloon and have me a nice cold beer.'

'Sounds good, Professor,' Dace addressed Bernard with the title he had given him for his fancy way of talking.

Bernard had grown used to the nickname. 'I never did thank you properly for stopping Moose McCune from taking me apart like a wooden doll that first week I was inside these walls. I'm still perplexed, why do you think he attacked me?'

'Dunno,' Dace replied. 'Never asked him about it.'

'It was good fortune they changed his work location,' Professor continued on the same subject. 'I fear he might have caught me when you weren't around to save the day.'

'Remember to thank the warden for moving him to the other side.'

Professor grinned. 'I'm still amazed at how easily you dispatched that immense brute. He is half again your size.'

'A bully sometimes isn't ready for an

immediate response.'

'I am still in your debt. In all probability he would have killed me.'

'Might have.'

'One of the guards told me he had gotten a letter the day before he came looking to do me bodily harm. It was the first letter he had received in two years. I can only wonder if he attacked me on someone's order.'

'It's possible.'

Professor frowned at him. 'My word, Dace! Do you ever express yourself with more than a syllable or two at a time? Eighteen months I've been here and I don't recall you ever putting two sentences together.'

'You talk enough for both of us.'

Professor flashed his good-natured grin. 'I confess I am given to verbosity now and again, but I'm a newspaper reporter.' He shrugged. 'Well, I was about to become one before I got sent here. I had my first big story ready to print not a week before my little mishap. It's still hard to believe the judge gave me a year-and-a-half sentence for starting one little fire. After all, I didn't do it on purpose.'

'Whose wife were you with at the time?' Dace reminded Professor of the circumstances.

'You're correct, Dace. If it hadn't been the mayor's wife and if the fire hadn't also burned down the schoolhouse when I knocked over the lamp . . . '

'Threw a boot at it to douse the light,' Dace again filled in the story.

'Well, it was either that or allow the mayor a clear shot! The man was pointing his pistol right at my . . . well, a bit below the belt.' Before Dace could add a remark he elaborated, 'Or where my belt would have been if I'd have had my pants on.'

'You going back to Golden?'

Professor snorted. 'Not in this lifetime. I intend to survive at least one more birthday.'

'You paid for the mistake.'

'I'm not sure a few months in prison

will be satisfactory for Mayor Ellis. He kicked his wife out when her indiscretion came to light. It was impossible to conceal the circumstances of my burning down the school at my hearing. Anyway, I'm sure I would not be welcomed back in Golden or the entire Denver area.'

'Maybe Ellis is the one who sent the letter to Moose?'

'It would be sheer speculation on my part to assume such, Dace. However, a few months after I arrived in this state institution, one of the infrequent newspapers they pass around had an article stating the mayor's wife had committed suicide. Perhaps her demise has satiated his desire for revenge.'

'Real shame she took her own life.'

'I suppose it could have been the public humiliation and a guilty conscience over being unfaithful.'

Dace grunted. 'Thanks to you.'

'I readily accept culpability for my actions, though I was not the first man sweet Melody Ellis wooed outside of

5

her marriage. Rex Ellis was a man of many faces. He won the election to mayor with a smile and saccharine promises, but I saw the bruises on his wife's body from his abuse.'

'He shares the blame for her death.'

'As do I,' Professor volunteered dolefully.

'You said she had been with other men?'

'At least one,' Steward replied. 'The poor chap perished in a fire.'

'Professor,' Dace said in exasperation, 'I used to think of you as an intelligent man. But anyone who messes with the wife of a rich and powerful mayor is stacking dry-grass hay in the middle of a firestorm!'

Professor grinned. 'Did I mention the lady was incredibly attractive?'

Dace sighed in defeat, ending the exchange as they had reached Warden Hayward's office. The guard, a man named Granger, who had been leading the way during their conversation, pushed open the door.

6

'Kelly and Perkins, Warden,' he announced.

'Bring them in.'

Dace didn't know why he had been summoned, but he didn't mind the short trip. It had given him a chance to say goodbye to Professor.

The warden was a mellow gent whose rules were to be followed to the letter and he expected the prisoners to behave. On the humane side, he wasn't above reprimanding a guard if they were too rough, or got carried away when chastizing a prisoner. His philosophy was that every man or woman sent to prison should learn a lesson and suffer enough punishment so they never wanted to come back, but he did not endorse or tolerate beatings or torture.

'I've your release papers here, Bernard,' Hayward said. 'I hope you'll take this new lease on life and make something of yourself other than a jackass.'

Professor held up his right hand as if swearing an oath. 'No more married women for me, Warden. My feet are set on the straight and narrow path from this day forward.'

'You can collect your things at the main gate. Granger will escort you from here.'

Professor accepted his note of pardon and stepped back. However, he didn't leave the room, but waited for the warden to speak to Dace.

Hayward ignored his presence and put a steady look on Dace. 'I take a keen interest in each of my inmates here, Kelly. After reviewing your case, I believe an eight-year sentence was an excessive degree of punishment. On your behalf, I wrote to the governor and asked him to reduce your sentence.'

Dace didn't hide his surprise at the news. 'I'm much obliged,' he said.

'It took a little extra convincing, so I made a deal with him.'

'A deal, Warden?'

The man took a moment to put his thoughts in order. When he spoke, his genuine concern was obvious.

'My sister's husband, Eldon Greer, was killed a few months ago . . . found him with a broken neck and a turned-over wagon.' His features hardened. 'The sheriff down that way ruled it an accident, but my sister thinks he was murdered. She has a stepson to help manage the ranch, but he was crippled some years back. He handles the books for her, but he can't ride or help with the physical stuff.'

'What does Dace's incarceration have to do with any of that?' Professor asked.

Hayward flashed a mind-your-own-business look at Bernard and continued with the proposal. 'There is a rancher who has been trying to get his hands on the Greer place ever since he arrived in the same valley. He owns the law and has built up a sizeable ranch himself. My sister's place controls the only route through the mountain range further south and she lets anyone use it for free. With many of the canyon roads and bridges charging a toll these days, she could make a lot of money by doing the same.' He paused to tap his fingers on the desk. 'I can't leave my position here to run down there and see she doesn't get pushed off her land, but I'm her only living relative.'

'You want Dace to look into it!' Professor surmised. 'Because he's the man who provided retribution for the Tanner gang and dispatched seven of them to Boot Hill!'

'Bernard Perkins! If you can't be quiet, I'll have Granger drag you out of here.'

'The Tanner gang was personal,' Dace told the warden. 'They killed my dad and younger brother, along with his wife, when they burned them out. Everyone in the county knew the gang was responsible for a dozen other farmers or ranchers being killed over the period of a year or less.'

'So you left your job as a Denver gunsmith and sought justice!' the warden declared.

'The judge called it *revenge* when he announced my sentence.'

'Yes, but the ruling was manslaughter, not murder. He could have sentenced you to hang.'

'He could have called it self-defense too,' Dace countered. 'Every one of those men died with a gun in their hand, trying to kill me.'

'The hole card is this, Kelly,' Warden Hayward said. 'The governor has signed off on your early release, if you agree to go to Tolerance and sort out the trouble there. Finding a peace officer to send is like trying to scratch your ear with your elbow: it's you or nobody.'

'We'll go!' Professor spoke up for Dace. 'You've got our word on it, Warden. Dace and I will travel to Tolerance and settle their petty disputes. Dace can sort out the difficulties and I'll write it up for the nearest newspaper. We'll make a splendid team!'

'We'll match up like an elephant and a burro pulling in double-harness,' Dace quipped.

'This is a parole, not a pardon, Kelly,'

the warden explained. 'If you can put an end to the trouble in Tolerance, the governor will sign off on an unconditional release. If, however,' he warned, 'you should decide to run or get into more trouble, you could end up right back here serving out the entire eight-year sentence.'

'I understand,' Dace acknowledged.

'Put your faith in us, Warden,' Professor said quickly.

Hayward frowned at him. 'You don't have *raison d'être* for accompanying Kelly.'

Professor laughed. 'Bet you thought you would stump me with that expression, didn't you, Warden?'

For the first time since arriving in his office Hayward smiled. 'I spent two years at college before I landed a job as an assistant warden. I might even wind up teaching at the School of Minds one day.'

'Not me,' Professor was quick to respond, 'I intend to become a noted journalist or writer. Once I get a start,

I'll open my own newspaper or publishing house.'

'Footsteps of your father,' Hayward approved. 'I wish you well in your quest.'

'So is Kelly free to go?'

The warden leaned back in his chair and peered up at Dace. 'You haven't actually said you were accepting the arrangement.'

'I reckon it won't hurt to ride over to Tolerance and take a look at the situation,' Dace told him. 'I'll do what I can.'

'Your word is good enough for me,' Hayward said, rising from his chair. He extended his hand. 'I wish you luck.'

Dace took his hand in a firm grip. Right move or wrong, smart or ill-advised, he would be glad to get out of Canyon City.

Granger led the two of them down a corridor and eventually to the guard station next to the main gate. When their possessions were returned, Professor's concern was mostly that he had his prized ring back.

'From my father,' he told Dace. 'Twenty-two years a newspaper man until his heart stopped beating. See the engraving inside?' He rotated the ring but the writing was too small for Dace to read. 'It's Latin and means 'truth above bias' or the equivalent.'

'A proper motto for a newspaper man,' Dace said.

Professor slipped the gold ring on a finger on his right hand. 'A bit less snug than when I got here. Difficult to believe I lost weight, considering the exquisite cuisine they serve at the dining hall.'

'You're going to need that sense of humor, riding with Kelly,' Granger told Professor. 'Sounds like you're heading for a range war or something.'

Professor displayed his natural grin. 'No fortitude, no front page is my motto.'

'Good luck,' Granger said in return. 'I hope you don't get your head shot off.'

Dace gave the writer a solemn look. 'Granger could be right, Professor. If I'm heading for a range war, you'll be caught in the middle.'

'My path is set, my good friend, and I accept the risks.'

His words prompted Dace to give a nod of his head. 'All right then, let's put this place behind us.'

2

Grover Mackenzie stepped out from the bank and stared across the street. Suzanne Greer had stopped her one-horse buggy in front of the general store. Had it been transmittable, his heated gaze would have burned a hole in her back as she climbed down from the rig. The mere sight of her caused his blood to simmer and a tightness to spread throughout his chest. She had everything he wanted and the snooty little witch hadn't done a blessed thing to earn it!

He loathed the way she drew glances of admiration as she moved with the ease and natural grace of a lady. He reluctantly admitted her gait was more flattering than the way some of the farmer women plodded along like cattle. Heavy work shoes, too many kids and too many hours doing a man's work eliminated the subtle sway of a woman's hips. Were he ten years younger he might have tried to woo the lady rather than dominate or intimidate her.

Grover swore under his breath at the notion. Beauty was fleeting; power and affluence were what separated ordinary men from kings. From the time he first acquired a measure of wealth, he enjoyed the way people groveled at his feet and cowered when he bellowed an order.

That's my kind of respect — get out of the way or get stepped on!

However, things had not been going his way since coming to this valley. Every plan he had put in motion to gain the control and power he desired had failed. Suzanne should have been thrilled to sell her ranch — leastways the portion old man Miller had left to Eldon Greer upon his death. The combined ranches were too big for her to handle and she had only four men and a crippled boy to help. He had made her a good offer, but she threw it back into his face. He cursed her again for wanting to hold on to such a massive spread.

Perhaps she sought to remain true to her husband's legacy, yet he knew she had never loved Eldon Greer. Grover had done some digging and learned the facts behind her coming to Tolerance. Eldon's charm was not responsible for her decision to stay in the valley. And the wedding between them had been a sham, a ploy to dismiss the scandal of a young woman living alone with the man and his son. Eldon had been wholly devoted to his dead wife, plus he was fifteen years older than Suzanne. No, there had been no romantic love between them.

Even so, she won't give in, not so long as she thinks of me as her enemy!

He heard steps behind him and turned to see the sheriff on the walkway. 'Hey, Mac,' the worth-nothing lawman greeted him, 'how's it going today?'

18

Grover tore his eyes away from the store and faced Chuck Lawry. The man wore his usual twin Colts and expensive Stetson hat with a narrow silver band around the crown. When he smiled it revealed his uneven, tobacco-stained teeth.

'It appears Mrs Greer is picking up some supplies from the store,' Grover eventually responded. 'Got to give her credit, trying to manage that place with only a crippled kid to help.'

Chuck gave a shake of his head. 'Yup, I don't think that lady intends t' give up a single acre of her ranch. You done picked one tough she-cat t' try and bamboozle out of the right-of-way through Miller's Gap.'

'She'll come around,' Grover said quietly. 'It's difficult working against a woman, especially one who is well thought of by everyone in the valley. It's going to take a little longer than I expected, but I'll gain control of Miller's Gap in the end.'

'I was talking t' Kendall last night at

the saloon,' Chuck said, referring to Grover's ranch foreman, 'and he said you're starting the fall roundup. He says you don't have near enough cattle t' pay all the bills.'

'Money is going to be tight this year,' Grover admitted.

'I been meaning t' ask yuh about them three special hires yuh done brung in. They don't never do much of nuthin' . . . 'cept sit around at the saloon and play cards. Don't hardly seem like they're earning their keep.'

'I'll have more use for them during roundup.' Grover evaded any other information about their jobs. 'They look rough around the edges, but they know a little about cattle.'

'Makes a guy wonder how Mrs Greer does it, only four hired hands t' run a spread twice the size of yourn.'

'She usually hires some extra men when the roundup is under way. And don't forget, those four men on her payroll are all top hands. Kendall once said he would trade two of our riders for any one of them.'

'You're sure 'nuff right about that,' Chuck agreed. 'If she didn't have them there *vaqueros*, the place would fall down around her ears.'

'I'm hoping the lady will come around to my way of thinking one of these next days. That big-ranch is too much for her and young Nathan to operate.'

Chuck narrowed his gaze, looking Grover right in the eye. 'Guido claims they've had a number of cattle stolen the last coupla seasons.'

'I wouldn't know about that,' Grover replied carefully. 'I don't spend a lot of time out at the Greer ranch.'

'Makes me glad I'm a town sheriff. Was I working as a county lawman, I would have t' check out the rustling angle.' He snorted. 'Good way t' get kilt, sneaking around behind the bushes, trying t' discover whose altering brands with a running iron, or catch some cowboys in the act of rustling cattle.'

Grover waved a hand to dismiss the subject. 'I've seen a few altered brands over the years, Chuck. It wouldn't take a genius to recognize if Mrs Greer's G brand was made into an M. It would be sloppy work at best. An honest brand inspector would pick it out in a glance.'

'Yup, I heared they was getting tougher on fellows dealing in stolen cattle.'

'New laws have been passed concerning restrictions and rules on fresh brands. There's owner and brand registration, records being kept and checked upon delivery — everything has changed,' Grover explained. 'It's nearly impossible to pass off stolen and rebranded cattle these days'

'I'll take your word for it, Mac,' Chuck said, 'but it's still a shame yuh can't get control of Miller's Gap. Seems a waste to allow all the travel through that narrow gorge whilst no one makes a dime. I'll bet those smaller ranches down south would pay plenty to keep from having t' travel a hundred miles to go around.'

'That's how I see it too, Chuck,' Grover said.

This time Chuck did drop the topic. 'Me and some of the boys are gonna get us a table at the saloon tonight and play some cards. Yuh want t' sit in?'

'I've got an errand to run this evening. If you see Smoker, tell him to meet me at the livery an hour before sunset. Have him harness the big sorrel to my shay.'

'I kin have Keyes let him know for yuh. He's in town — over at the saloon.' He paused. 'Would yuh just as soon use Keyes?'

'No, Smoker's the man I want for tonight.'

'I'll have him pass the word,' Chuck said, lifting a hand in farewell. 'See yuh later . . . or maybe tomorrow.'

Grover might have said something more to him in reply but he didn't wish to keep the conversation going. He returned to looking after Suzanne Greer, wishing he knew a weakness to use against her. It didn't help that she distrusted him — the right term was contempt, because she thought him responsible for Eldon's death.

Her aged, pretended husband had suffered a fall which broke his neck as cleanly as if it had been the handiwork of Topper Perry, a massive brute who worked out at the Big M Ranch. Of course, the accident *had* been planned, and Topper *had* done the deed, but only Suzanne and Nathan Greer continued to voice their suspicions concerning his death. Chuck, dunce that he was, had taken one look at the scene and deduced it had been a wagon mishap.

Grover felt a hint of helpless frustration but dismissed it. He had to keep emotion aside if he was going to win the prize. A man who acted with his head won more often than the one who acted from his heart. He would deal with Nathan, if the young man became too much of a problem. He had men on his payroll who would do any job given to them. It was only a matter of time before he got what he wanted.

Considering his hired men, Top Perry was not much of a thinking man but he followed orders and kept his mouth shut. Vince Kendall had been a good choice for managing his ranch. He was honest enough not to steal or make false entries in the books, plus he worked for less money because he enjoyed having a house for his wife and kids. Up to this point, he had also been smart enough not to question how Grover continued to finance the ranch. Then there was Wayde, the man in charge of the wranglers and cowpunchers. He was more cattleman than gunman, but knew the ins and outs of using a running iron. Keyes was his number two man, willing to follow orders and use his gun if necessary. His one fault was being envious of Smoker's position. Next, he had the trio of hired guns, his rustling crew, who always stayed available in town. Considering he had more than a dozen riders out at the ranch, it was hard to believe the Greer ranch could get by with only four regular hands. Of course, that made it easier for Grover's thieves to steal cattle without being caught.

Lastly, there was Smoker, his most valuable asset. With his name on several state or territory wanted posters, Grover had bailed the man out of a jam and won an ally. He trusted Smoker to do the special jobs that needed discreet handling.

Within the town of Tolerance, no one readily opposed Grover's will. The sheriff basically worked for him and didn't ask a lot of questions. The mayor, Jason Dower, owned the general store. He was the kind of man who wanted a measure of self respect, yet had never dared pit himself opposite of Grover. The other businessmen around town enjoyed the money his men spread around and adopted an *ignorance is bliss* philosophy. He had control of the valley except for the one thing he needed most — Miller's Gap!

Grover patted his pocket, remembering his reason for the trip to the bank. He had tapped the last of his credit. The bank was also the freight office and handled the mail and telegraph. The bank manager was new in town, a nobody who had to seek approval from his home bank in Denver before lending money. Banking posed a problem because Grover had taken an original loan on the deed to his ranch, one which listed the number of cattle. He couldn't overstate the growth of his herd without bringing suspicion upon himself. If he was audited, it would be impossible to explain how his original 300 head of cattle had managed to average two calves each over the past two years. No one in the cattle business would believe that!

Grover cursed his luck at having arrived in the valley last. He had been forced to settle for the mountainous northern range for his ranch. It had less feed and water than the other two big ranches. Old man Miller originally owned the central portion and controlled the only pass for a hundred miles around. Smoker had seen to it the man died in a hunting mishap, but

Miller had double-crossed Grover in death. He had listed Eldon Greer as his beneficiary! Greer had wound up with twice as many cattle and gained control of Miller's Gap. Grover agonized over that turn of events. With the added cattle, Greer was that much more dug in and Eldon had refused to sell even a portion of Miller's old place. In order to break Greer, it was necessary to hire more high-priced gunmen and steal enough cattle to keep from going broke.

He laughed at the ridiculous situation. In his younger days, he had opted not to fight in the war between the Union and the Confederacy. Instead, he had found ways to make money selling items both sides needed. A consignment of food or medical supplies was not as closely guarded as a payroll, so he and a couple of other outlaws had been able to steal several shipments and resell them to the opposite side. A good businessman knew the only real winners in a war were those who found a way to make a profit. Let the suckers die for a cause. He had risked everything to gain control of Miller's Gap. Now he was backed into a corner, financially depleted, and forced to do whatever it took to get what he wanted. He set his teeth hard, bitter at the idea of Suzanne Greer and her crippled partner blocking his way to wealth and power. They were not going to stop him for much longer, even if it meant the death of them both!

★ ★ ★

Nathan thanked Suzanne for preparing the evening meal, something he had started doing after Eldon died, and retired to the sitting-room. She knew he would be engrossed reading a recent copy of the *Police Gazette* or one of his penny dreadful stories. It was sad to watch him hobble about, as he had a hard time getting around. She wondered how much different he would have been had he been able to run, work and play as a young man, rather than sit back and watch the world as a prisoner in his own body.

She cleared away the dishes and began to wash the plates. Occupying her hands did not cause her thoughts to cease. Considering how different Nathan's life might have been caused her to wonder about her own. If she hadn't agreed to move to Tolerance to tend to a crippled young man, if Eldon had not been so kind and caring, would she now be in a completely different life? With the sudden violent death of her mother, Suzanne was left alone in the world. It was the circuit parson who knew about Eldon and Nathan Greer. With several small towns on his route, he had led a prayer meeting in Tolerance and met up with the pair. He was nice enough to write a letter of introduction for Suzanne and she ended up moving to Tolerance a few weeks later.

Nathan had suffered his injury at the tender age of twelve, when his cow pony fell during roundup and the boy was trampled by several excited steers. When Suzanne arrived at the ranch, the boy could barely sit up on his own. Suzanne recalled the first few months of working with him. It had been a trying experience for both she and Nathan. He didn't want to be a cripple and she didn't know how much to do for him. They fought at first, each trying to gauge the other's degree of control or authority. Once they mutually accepted the position of the other, they ceased battling and began to work together. Nathan had to learn to walk and even dress himself. Each stride of his progress was a shared victory, with both of them eager for him to succeed, each enthusiastic about testing his limits and trying to do even more.

With the measure of success, Nathan and Eldon made a trip to Denver to visit a noted surgeon. They departed with high hopes, only to return with the unhappy news; the nerve damage could not be reversed. Once his overall recovery was complete, Nathan was left with minimal use of his left arm and a severe limp whenever he walked. Being unable to do the strenuous work on the ranch, Eldon taught him to manage the bills, do the bookkeeping and take care of the payroll.

It was after her third year with the two men that Eldon suggested they marry. His biggest fear was something might happen to him and Nathan would be left all alone. With Suzanne as his legal wife, she could manage or sell the place and see his son was taken care of. Eldon had no romantic notions about her, having come to think of her as his own daughter. He was also fifteen years her senior, but he knew she and Nathan had become as close as if they were brother and sister. Suzanne didn't want to leave the boy or the ranch, so she agreed.

Suzanne had been Eldon's wife for a little over a year when tragedy struck. His sudden and unexpected death had hit both of them hard, a heartbreak from which they were still trying to recover.

'We've got company,' Nathan spoke up from the next room, interrupting her reverie. 'Sounds like a wagon or buggy just pulled into the front yard.'

Suzanne quickly wiped her hands on the drying cloth and went to the front door. Stepping outside, it took only a glance to recognize Grover Mackenzie in the one-horse carriage. The man at his side was a fellow called Smoker, though she had never seen him with a lit cigarette.

'Don't bother to get up,' Suzanne spoke over her shoulder to Nathan. 'I'll tend to this.'

'OK, Sue.'

Being dusk, the world was thrown into shadows. Suzanne stepped out the front door and closed it behind her. Before Grover could get down, she strode over and stopped next to the carriage.

'I don't remember giving you an invite to come and visit, Mr Mackenzie.'

Grover smiled down at her. 'Suzanne,

honey, why do you continue to treat me like I've got the plague? You know I only want what is best for you.'

'That's reassuring,' she replied in a cynical tone. 'And here I thought you wanted to steal our ranch.'

Suzanne saw Smoker set the brake and hop down on the other side of the buggy. Before she could think of a way to be rid of them, Grover also climbed down.

'It seems you are lacking manners as well as proper hearing,' she told Grover curtly. 'What do you want?'

Grover stood directly in front of her and stared down into her face. 'I want you to think about my offer, Suzanne, honey,' he said provocatively. 'It's time we stopped playing games and came to terms.'

'Terms?' She grew sarcastic. 'If you would kindly drop dead, I'll pay to see you buried. How about those terms?'

Grover remained poised, his eyes travelling over her, a blatant act of intimidation. She held herself rigid, battling a tremor of trepidation. This was her land, her home — she refused to cower from this man.

'You're in over your head here, Suzanne,' he said huskily. 'You can't run a ranch this size all alone.'

'I have Nathan and my ranch hands,' she replied. 'I'm not alone.'

Before she grasped his intentions, Grover reached out and gripped her by the upper arms. A grim desperation shone naked on his face.

'Damn your haughty attitude, Suzanne!' he said, his voice rising an octave. 'I've offered you a good price to sell, or a partnership which will keep you well off for the rest of your life! You can have everything your heart desires! Why can't you understand I'm trying to do what is best for both of us?'

'Let go of me!' she said sharply.

'Not until you listen to what I have to say!'

The door opened and Nathan appeared with a pistol in his good hand. He pointed it at Grover. 'Get your hands off of my sister!' he shouted.

But Smoker came out of the shadows like a ghost. He struck down on Nathan's wrist and threw his shoulder into him. The gun went flying from Nathan's fist and, when he attempted to regain his balance, Smoker shoved him roughly to the ground.

'Stop it!' Suzanne cried. 'Leave him alone!'

Grover jerked her up against his chest and glared down at her. 'Wake up, Suzanne!' he sneered, his fingers biting into the flesh of her upper arms. 'You can't fight me! I'm going to have this place with or without you selling out!'

Rather than reply, Suzanne snaked her hand up and clawed Grover along the side of his face. The violent action prompted a sudden and brutal response.

3

'Behold, the ranch stands before us,' Professor said happily. 'I calculated we'd make it by dark.'

'You're a genius,' Dace allowed.

'Well, it was quite simple . . . approximate miles divided by approximate speed equals the approximate time needed to cross the measured distance.'

'An exact timetable, if ever I heard one,' Dace remarked drily.

Professor laughed. 'Truthfully, I expected to sleep under the stars again tonight.'

The landscape was darkening, but they could make out several outbuildings, a corral and the main house — two windows showed lights — and there was a buggy in the yard.

'Something happening there,' Dace told his pal. 'Looks like some kind of tussle going on by the buggy.'

'Perchance we are intruding upon

someone's privacy. It could be young lovers romantically entwined.'

At that moment, the larger shadow slapped the smaller one across the face! Dace instantly put heels to his horse. The bolting forward of his mount caught Professor by surprise.

'Hold on! What's the . . . ?' Then Professor kicked his own animal into a run to catch up.

Their hasty approach broke up the grappling between the two next to the carriage. Dace pulled his horse to an abrupt halt at the edge of the yard, where he could see four people clearly. One man was off to the side, standing over a young fellow on the ground, near the front of the house. Of the two facing him, a woman was gingerly rubbing her cheek, where she had been struck. The well-dressed gent, who had been scuffling with her, had fresh scratch marks on the side of his face.

'Evening, folks,' Dace said carefully, relaxing in the saddle, while subtly easing the thong from the hammer of his gun. 'Would this be the Greer ranch?'

'Who the hell are you?' The man wearing the expensive suit and fashionable felt businessman's hat, demanded impudently.

Dace paid no attention to him, touching the rim of his hat in a polite gesture toward the lady. 'Ma'am?'

'You're sticking your nose where it doesn't belong,' the fellow in the shadows spoke up, his voice as cool as the whisper of death. 'Might get yourself shot full of holes.'

Dace remained at ease, his hand resting on the butt of his pistol as if unintentional. He measured the man by the house — gun tied low, poised like a snake ready to strike. When the man moved into the light streaming from the front door, Dace could see his eyes shone with a reckless excitement. To move or twitch suddenly would be to start a deadly gunfight.

Before anyone could react or say another word, Professor broke the silence.

'A very good evening to all of you,' he piped up cheerfully. 'I'm Bernard Perkins and this is my traveling companion, Dace Kelly. We've been three days in the saddle to reach this most solitary valley, and though we are not affluent men, we would most certainly offer a nominal recompense for a cooked meal and a night's lodging.'

'Dace Kelly?' The semi-crouched gunman repeated the name. 'Not the Kelly who was sent to prison some years back?'

Professor sniffed and lifted his chin importantly. 'The very same,' he replied. 'Before you is the just avenger who eradicated the three Tanner brothers and four of their cohort gunmen over in Echo County a short three years back. I shouldn't want to provoke a man of his caliber,' he warned the shadowy figure, 'that is, unless you are carrying a last will and testament in your back pocket and wish to have it read shortly.'

'Smoker, you know of this joker?' asked the man with the scratched face.

'A hellion with a gun, Mr Mackenzie, if the newspapers told it straight.'

'Are you an escaped convict?' Mackenzie asked in a commanding tone of voice. 'What are you doing here?'

Dace ignored him for the second time and spoke to the woman. 'Would you be Mrs Greer?'

'She sure is!' the boy on the ground made his first contribution to the conversation. 'And I'm Nathan Greer. This here is our ranch.'

'Mr Mackenzie,' Mrs Greer bobbed her head at the man who had struck her, 'and his pet gunman were just leaving.'

Smoker moved effortlessly over to stand near Mackenzie. 'That the way it is, boss?' he queried, his eyes still fixed upon Dace. 'Are we leaving?'

The man in the suit seemed undecided for a moment. Dace maintained a calm and unperturbed expression, as if unconcerned about what the man decided one way or the other. Before Mackenzie could make his decision, the woman reached out and gave him a shove.

'Go on home, Grover,' she said. 'Don't make this any worse.'

'Think about what I said,' he told her, a veiled threat evident in his tone of voice. Smoker walked around and climbed into their carriage. Once Grover had joined him on the wagon seat, the pompous man put his attention on the lady and added, 'It's the best offer you will ever get.'

'Goodbye!' Mrs Greer said with a degree of finality. She waited as Grover flipped the reins to start his horse and the carriage circled and proceeded down the main trail. With the troublesome man gone, she hurried over to help Nathan get to his feet.

As soon as he was standing under his own power, Nathan made several awkward steps crossing the yard where he could take a better look at Dace.

'I don't believe it!' His voice exhibited his enthusiasm. 'Dace Kelly! The Lone Gunman of Echo Country. I read about you in the *Police Gazette*! You should have been given a medal, rather than being sent to prison.'

'A consensus mirrored by many,' Professor remarked. 'Personally, I've never met a more honorable man than the one beside me.'

'What do you want, Mr Kelly?' the woman asked brusquely, speaking to Dace. 'Why are you here?'

'Our presence is at the behest of your brother, Warden William Hayward,' Professor answered the question. 'He suggested you and your ranch might be in some peril.'

'We do not need a hired killer,' Mrs Greer responded icily. 'My brother should not have gotten involved.'

Professor was confounded, at a loss for words . . . probably a first for him. Dace hid a smile at the notion and politely tipped his hat.

'I beg your pardon, Mrs Greer,' he apologized. 'It wasn't our aim to cause you any distress.'

She held herself erect, more inflexible

than defiant. 'No killer with a gun is welcome on our land, Mr Kelly.'

'I understand.' He remained respectful. 'We'll be in town a few days, should you have a change of heart.'

Nathan whirled on the woman, almost losing his balance from the sudden movement. 'What are you doing, Sue?' he cried. 'Your brother sent them to help us!' He pointed at Dace. 'And there sits the one man who might be able to stand up to Grover and his band of cutthroats!'

'I'm sorry, Nate,' she spoke gently to him, 'but I won't have a killer like him on our ranch.'

Dace neck-reined his horse and started off in the same direction Mackenzie had taken. Professor hesitated only long enough to bid a 'good evening' to the pair in the yard, before he rode up alongside.

'Not the heartfelt greeting one might have expected,' he said, after they had ridden a short distance. 'And to think we arrived in time to aid fair damsel.

What a disappointment.'

'Life doesn't always follow the fairy-tale path writers put to paper.'

'Too true, Dace,' Professor admitted. 'However, it's a woeful development to travel so long to reach this introverted stretch of wilderness only to be swatted aside like unwanted flying pests! It's utterly mortifying.'

'Can't blame the lady for not wanting a gunman around.'

Professor emitted a sigh. 'Perhaps I should have returned to Golden and pursued the mystery surrounding Mayor Ellis.'

'Probably end up the victim of a questionable suicide like his ex-wife,' Dace stated.

'Alas, you are right. I shall continue my endeavors hereabouts for the time being. Considering someone wished me ill upon my arrival at Canyon City, it requires little reflection to conclude my journalistic talents will be more appreciated elsewhere.'

Dace continued the ride in silence.

He should have felt something over the Greer woman's rejection — relief, anger, even annoyance, but he had no emotions at hand. The life and compassion he had known in his youth had perished along with the deaths of his father and brother . . . and Anne.

Guilt assailed his conscience and a terrible ache gripped his heart. He battled against the pain, telling himself he had done the honorable thing. He had left home, gone off to find a life on his own. Only he knew the real reason for leaving the homestead . . . though he suspected Anne had guessed the truth.

Judge Roper had been correct in his ruling; the extreme retribution Dace had dealt to the Tanner brothers and their gang had been a personal vendetta, far more lethal than a desire to make them pay for their crime. In retrospect, he would do nothing different if given the chance. Every night since the brutal murders, whenever he lay down and closed his eyes, he envisioned his brother, his dad and Anne, their three unrecognizable bodies laid out for burial. He still endured seething hatred when dwelling upon their charred remains.

Always better than average with a gun, Dace had often shown off for his customers. He had sold many a gun by demonstrating the precision and speed a person could acquire with a little serious practise. When news reached him of the attack, he had turned his business over to the bank and returned home. Within a few weeks he had caught up to each and every one of the killers. Confronting them alone or in pairs, he dealt out a swift and deadly justice . . . revenge, Judge Roper had accurately proclaimed. There had been no law in Echo County, no one else to ask for help. If not for Dace, the Tanners would still be stealing property and killing innocent victims. Judge Roper had been sympathetic on that count but could not condone vigilante justice. He sentenced Dace to eight years . . . one year for each man he'd killed and another for destroying his own life.

After three years behind bars, Dace had no idea as to what the remainder of his life held in store for him. He was glad to be free, to be on the back of a horse and able to breathe the open air, but he lacked direction and purpose. A big part of him had died with his family; the remainder had withered away in prison. He was a hollow shell, a mere shadow of his former self.

'I don't embrace the role of pessimist, Dace, but what are we going to do in town?' Professor asked, breaking the quietness. 'My financial worth consists of six dollars and I must purchase supplies for my writing endeavors. I had assumed we would enjoy room and board, along with the probability of at least short-time employment.'

'I'm a fair hand at poker,' Dace replied. 'If I can sit in at a square game, I might be able to win us a small stake.'

'Yes, I recall you fleecing the guards a

time or two during our stay in Canyon City.'

'Too bad I spent most of my money to buy a horse and travel supplies.'

'Whatever happened to your father's place?'

'The Tanners sold the livestock and the house is nothing but a pile of ashes.'

'And your business enterprise in Denver?'

'The bank took it back when I decided to run down the Tanners. Like you, this horse and a few dollars is my entire worth at the moment.'

'Ah, yes, our thrilling adventure grows better with each step we take.'

'It was your idea to tag along,' Dace reminded him.

'I heard it said once that a man had to suffer before he could write from the heart.'

'Eighteen months behind bars and you are still worried about suffering?'

Professor laughed. 'Perhaps if you had not intervened on my behalf, when Moose McCune tried to attack me?'

'How many stories have been written by dead men?' Dace returned.

'You're right, of course. That brute would have torn me limb from limb, like trimming a branch for use as a fishing pole.'

Dace didn't respond.

'I am still amazed as to your fighting prowess,' Professor did not allow the silence to continue. 'It was over so quickly, I didn't even see what you did to him.'

'I call it cunning,' he answered, 'most men would call it fighting dirty.'

Professor chucked again. 'Whatever its label, one cannot argue the effectiveness of such tactics.'

'It helps to strike first too,' Dace admitted. 'Catch them unawares, before they know they are in a fight.'

'I shall try to remember that should I find myself in the same circumstance.'

They followed the trail until they spied the lighted windows of the town and a hanging lamp at the livery. Tolerance was not a large place, but it had more to offer than a crossroads trading post or weigh station. Several stores were visible, a saloon and even one two-storey building that had the word BANK painted on the upper deck.

They stopped at the livery, which also housed a forge for blacksmithing. Before they could dismount an elderly gent stepped out to greet them.

'Howdy, strangers,' he said, displaying a smile which revealed several missing front teeth. 'Welcome to Tolerance. Bartholomew Simpkins is the name — folks call me Bo.'

'Good evening, sir,' Professor spoke up in reply. 'I'm Bernard Perkins and my friend here is Dace Kelly.'

'Appears you've come a fair piece,' Bo said, looking over their mounts. 'Enough dust on them horses to plant a crop of corn.'

'Is there a boarding-house in town?'

Bo smiled again. 'My missus and I have the big house at the opposite end of town — there be three spare rooms we rent out. We like to say we get folks coming, staying and going.' He chuckled, as if he expected the next question and added. 'She don't cotton to the smell of horse manure is the reason I had to put my livery down here.'

'You are ingenious entrepreneurs,' Professor praised, 'servicing the needs of weary travelers as well as providing for their mode of conveyance.'

Bo regarded Professor as he might have a frog wearing feathers, but remained cordial. 'I was about to turn out the lamp for the night. If you boys want to put up your horses, I'll walk you to my house. Might be able to wrangle you a bit of supper that way.'

'If it's no trouble,' Dace told him.

'One meal a day is included with the price of a room, not counting breakfast. Fresh wheat toast and grits are provided every morning as a courtesy. I 'spect it's roast mutton tonight.'

'Sounds like gourmet cuisine!' Professor exclaimed. 'Let's dispense with these animals forthwith. I'm famished.'

* * *

There were three busy gaming tables at the saloon and a couple of men at the roulette wheel. Dace spent a few minutes sipping a beer and watching the different groups of players before deciding which table offered him the best odds of winning. When an empty chair presented itself, he asked and was invited to sit in. The four men consisted of a store owner, a Mexican cow puncher and two other men who worked around town. The game was quarterante and dollar limit for raises, a relatively inexpensive game. Within an hour Dace, playing a cautious game, was up by a little over ten dollars.

'What are your plans for the future, Mr Kelly?' Jason Dower asked, while shuffling the cards for a fresh deal. He owned the general store and was also the city mayor.

'I'm looking for work,' Dace replied. 'If I don't land something around here, I'll move on in a coupla days.'

'You might take up gambling for a living,' he suggested. 'You've had a bit of luck this evening.'

'Luck is too fickle,' Dace told him. 'I seldom win enough to more than pass the time. A good gambler stays in nice hotels and eats in the finest restaurants . . . I usually end up camped under the stars with a can of beans.'

'I like beans,' the Spanish gent spoke up, grinning. 'Give me beans and flour and I can cook you a feast.'

'You left out peppers,' Dace replied. 'Most Mexican food is too hot for my taste. I tried some chilli con carne one time where they had to keep putting a wet towel over the kettle to douse the flames.'

'Guido is my best customer when I get in some hot peppers,' Dower put in. 'I'd wager he and his cousins stay warmer than anyone else when the cold weather hits . . . so long as the peppers hold out.'

There was laughter all around. Guido stopped short when a shadow fell over his cards. Dace looked up to see a man with a shaved head and shoulders about as wide as a wagon bed. He towered over the table like a huge oak tree.

'Thought it was you I seen coming to town, Lopez.' The man spoke to Guido, his lips curled back like a growling dog and the light of mischief dancing in his eyes. 'I recognized the smell too.'

Lopez blanched, undoubtedly afraid of the giant, and said nothing.

'Easy, Topper,' Dower spoke up. 'We're just having us a friendly game of cards. Let's not have any trouble.'

The brute called Topper threw him a heated shut-your-mouth glare and again turned his rancor on Lopez. 'We don't want any trash coming in here from the Greer ranch. You and your cousins ain't welcome.' He showed another sneer. 'You best skedaddle before I drag you out of the saloon by your hair!'

Dace had seen the scenario before, the pushing and taunting, forcing someone into a fight they couldn't win. Topper had come to the saloon with the single purpose of pulverizing the man he called Lopez.

'No one invited you to butt in on our game, big mouth,' Dace calmly told the big man. 'Why don't you meander down to the nearest pig sty and visit your relatives.'

Topper's mouth fell open. 'What'd you say?'

'Well, I can't believe you got those hog jowls and snout from human parents,' Dace jeered. He shook his head as if incredulous. 'Damn, it must have been one revolting sow to have given birth to a muscle-headed oaf like you.'

Topper stomped around the table to confront Dace. He planted his legs like twin tree trunks and placed his hands on his thick hips. 'On your feet, wiseacre!' he roared. 'I'm going to shower the floor with your blood!'

Dace swung suddenly about, still in the chair, and viciously struck out with his boot heel, cracking Topper square on the knee cap. The immediate shock caused him to howl in pain and double over, reaching for the injured leg. Lunging upward, Dace jabbed with the knuckles on his right hand, striking the man in his Adam's apple hard enough to cut off his air supply.

Topper staggered back a step, both hands now on his throat. Before he had a chance to defend himself, Dace used the heel of his hand to smack the man's nose, jamming it upward at the same time. The quick and lethal combination drove the brute backwards. He slammed hard against the bar and slid down to a sitting position.

Dace pounced like a cat, straddling him, pinning his head back against the counter with his forearm, poised to smash him full in the face with his doubled fist.

'I can do you a lot of damage, my porky friend,' he hissed the words. 'You came here to start trouble, but do you really want a fight?'

Topper could not get air into his lungs. His eyes bugged, his face flamed red, while he gasped and choked, sucking barely enough air to keep from passing out.

'Make your decision, big man!' Dace remained ready to strike.

Topper slowly turned his head from side to side, struggling to gulp air into his lungs, as blood began to trickle from his broken nose.

Dace rose up and stepped back. He quickly searched the room in case someone had the notion to come to Topper's defense. No one had moved; the entire room was filled with a stunned silence. Satisfied the short fracas was finished, he resumed his place at the card table and, once seated again, looked passively around at the other players.

'I forget, whose deal is it?'

4

Suzanne was surprised to find Nathan already up, dressed and seated at the table. Before she could ask about his becoming such an early riser, he opened the conversation.

'Guido went to town last night,' he began. 'It was a fool stunt to go alone, but you know how he is.'

'Oh, no!' she lamented, fearing something dreadful had happened.

'Top Perry came looking for trouble. He found Guido at the saloon and tried to goad him into a fight.'

'That big brute is twice Guido's size!' she exclaimed fearfully. 'Is he . . . is he all right?'

'Dace Kelly took on Perry by himself.'

Suzanne caught her breath. 'Dace Kelly, but . . . ?'

'Guido says Kelly knocked the big

oaf to the floor and had him pinned before anyone in the place knew there was a fight. He never touched his gun yet moved so quickly; Guido didn't even see how he did it.'

'You think he did this for us because my brother sent him here to help,' she stated.

'According to Guido, he hadn't told Kelly that he worked for us. He stood up for a man he had barely met to save him from a beating, that's it.'

'The man is a gunman.' Suzanne continued to be critical. 'Gunmen have no consideration for anyone but themselves. He must have known Guido worked for us.'

'He didn't know,' Nathan maintained. 'And he didn't use a gun, or do permanent damage to Top Perry either. Guido said the big lout got up under his own power and limped out of the room after a few minutes.' Nathan let out a deep breath, 'I think it was a mistake to send Kelly away.'

'Do you want to get into a bloody

range war with Mackenzie?' she challenged. 'How long do you think we would last against his hired guns?'

Nathan did not back down. 'How long are we going to last doing nothing, Sue? We've lost over a hundred head of cattle this year; Grover and his men keep pushing, and now they come right into the yard and he starts manhandling you! When does it stop?'

'There are limits to how far Grover will go, Nate. He has to live in the valley and he doesn't own everyone.'

'He's had it in his head to gain control of Miller's Gap ever since he arrived in Tolerance and he's going to do whatever it takes to get it.'

Suzanne would have argued, but she knew Nathan was right. When she spoke, the resignation came into her voice. 'What would you have me do, Nate? I can't go to the new gunman in town and beg him to come help us.'

'Your brother already asked him,' Nathan reminded her. 'That's why he's here in the valley . . . to help us.'

Suzanne sat down at the table and her shoulders bowed under the weight of responsibility. She hadn't asked for a husband; nor for a younger step-brother — she had never been able to think of Nathan as her son; and the ranch was a much bigger burden than she had imagined. All things combined, it was a much harder task than she was physically or mentally able to cope with.

'My mother was going to the store to pick up a few things,' she began a story. 'About the same time, a trio of gunmen decided to rob the saloon. She was an innocent bystander on the main street in town when a bullet struck her in the chest.' Suzanne lowered her head, the memory a deep ache in her heart. 'Moments later my mother lay dead, while the gunmen rode out of town and were never caught. They killed the saloon owner and a second man during the holdup, then shot my mother simply because she was passing by. I can't forget her death; how she was killed by men just like Dace Kelly.'

'I understand your hatred of killers like those men, Sue,' Nathan said gently, 'but Dace Kelly isn't some soulless gunman. He didn't take up a gun to be feared or intimidate people, he did it because there was no law in Echo County.'

'He killed over a half-dozen men. You said so yourself.'

'I read the account in the *Police Gazette*. Those were the very men who had murdered his father and brother, along with his brother's wife. They set fire and burned his home to the ground and it's possible one or more of the victims were still alive at the time. Dace Kelly dealt out justice.'

'He ended up in jail.'

'What would you do if you knew where to find the three men who killed your mother?' Nathan changed the subject. 'What if the law couldn't or wouldn't touch them? Would you forget about them? Would you say it's just how things are and be satisfied to let them go unpunished?'

'You're suggesting I would hire someone to kill them?'

Nathan sighed. 'If I knew for certain Pa was murdered and didn't die by accident, I'd darn well want someone to deal out justice.'

'That's what Dace Kelly did and he ended up behind bars.'

'Where your brother got to know him!' Nathan added to her statement. 'Do you really think William would send a man here if he thought you were going to hate him without first giving him a chance?'

'I haven't spoken to Bill since our mother's funeral. He was not living at home at the time.'

'You said once how he invited you to come and live with him.'

'He already had a wife and baby,' Suzanne replied. 'I didn't want to be a burden.'

Nathan took on a very serious look. 'You came here instead, so you could take care of me. Guess that makes me the burden instead of you.'

'You've never been a burden, Nate.'

'And you took marriage vows to keep people from gossiping and to drive the other suitors away too,' he continued. 'You have sacrificed your life for me and our ranch.'

'I found a new home,' she argued.

'Because you pitied me!'

'No!' she snapped at him. 'I'm sorry about your accident, but I've never felt pity for you. I'm impressed by how you accepted your limitations and keep on trying. I marvel at the improvement you've made, by your optimistic and cheery attitude, by the way you accept responsibility and continually try to do more than your share around the ranch! You are more like a brother to me than Bill ever was. With him being ten years older than me I hardly knew him.'

Nathan could not hide a smile. 'You've always been defensive about my limitations. Even when you have to help me in or out of a wagon — I've seen how you glare at people to keep them from teasing or saying something.'

'That's what a big sister should do.'

He grew serious. 'And I need to do something too, Sue. I've been managing the books since my father died. You've never shown much interest in learning that part of the ranch business.'

'You have a good head for sums and Eldon said you did a good job of keeping records. Why should I need to know any more about that side of the ranch?'

'Because we are on the road to failure.' Nathan watched for her reaction. She gaped in shock and he explained. 'We've got less than fifty steers to send to market at the end of the month. Luis gave me the count the other day. There can be no doubt rustlers have stolen most of our marketable cattle.'

Suzanne clenched her jaw. 'I'll wager no one has rustled any cattle from Mackenzie's place.'

'No, and it's no surprise how his original two or three hundred head of cattle more than doubled the first year he arrived. Guido overheard a couple of riders talking about his cattle and at his herd's rate of growth. His cows don't have single calves, they have litters like rabbits.'

'He's behind the rustling.'

'And the only law around is a town sheriff on his payroll,' Nathan added. 'If we don't have a better spring round-up, we're going to have to start cutting our help.'

'Other than during roundup we've only got the four regular hands now!' she cried. 'It would be impossible to manage the ranch with fewer men.'

'When Miller left his place to Pa, we had over a thousand head of cattle. I doubt we have half that many now.'

Suzanne wrung her hands. 'We can't lose the ranch.'

'We have two things going for us,' Nathan pointed out. 'Pa always did business directly with the bank at Denver, and so long as his old friend is the bank manager there, we can work out a way to make the mortgage payments. And because we write bank drafts on our Denver account, we are able to pay our bills and Mackenzie has no way of knowing how much money we have.'

'From the way you're talking, it isn't enough.'

'Not if we want to eat more than once a week and keep our four underpaid cow punchers on the payroll.'

'And you count this as being in our favor?'

Nathan shrugged. 'It's important we keep our finances a mystery . . . for the time being anyway. I'm sure Mackenzie would love to know we can't make the next payment and get through the winter without selling at least a hundred head of beef. If he was able to take over our mortgage, he would quickly find a reason to foreclose and legally take the place away from us. You know it wouldn't be but a few days later and he would have his toll road in operation.'

'Toll . . . another word for extortion.'

'Yeah, it's not as if anyone built a

bridge or bored a tunnel through the side of a mountain. It was a trail Miller found when several head of his cattle went missing — a few felled trees and a day or two moving boulders with a strong team of horses. He didn't think it was worth charging anyone to use the trail and we've been able to join our herd with those cattlemen from the south every year since they started coming this way.'

'I can imagine what Grover would charge for using the pass — two-bits for every cow, horse, sheep or person . . . double for a wagon.'

'He's a blood-sucker all right.'

'You said we had two things going for us,' Suzanne reminded him. 'What is the second?'

Nathan made a face as if he expected her to not like his next answer.

'Dace Kelly.'

Suzanne's negative reaction was immediate. 'Uh-uh, Nate, we can't involve Kelly. I don't want a range war. I'll speak to the boys and ask them to do a better job of protecting our cattle. The rustlers have never attacked our riders.'

'If Mackenzie gets desperate, there's no telling what he will do.'

'Then we'll deal with it when the time comes.' She remained adamant. 'I won't have some wild-eyed killer working on our ranch.' With more force she repeated, 'I won't!'

'The guy was pretty cool-headed when he faced Smoker.' Nathan defended the man he had read about. 'And Guido said Dace never raised his voice when he knocked Top Perry flat on his back pockets.'

'That isn't the point,' Suzanne argued. 'If we let him stay here on the ranch there will be bloodshed. I don't want to be the one who initiates a war.'

'Stealing half of our herd makes it plain the war started when Mackenzie came to the valley, Sue.'

'The answer is no!' she said emphatically.

Nathan was practically full grown, but Suzanne was the senior partner in their arrangement. Stepmother or step-sister, she was the one who had the final word.

* * *

The man had a tin star pinned to his vest, wore two guns and had a strut to his walk. Dace knew a haughty rooster when he saw one, and this cocky son was headed his way. He didn't pretend not to see him, but turned and waited until the man approached.

'Kelly, isn't it?' the sheriff asked.

'That's right.'

He tipped back his twenty-dollar hat and put on a stern expression. Dace supposed it might have intimidated a young kid or some green pilgrim. However, he had spent the last three years meeting a lot tougher stares than the one from this clown.

'I'm Chuck Lawry,' he tapped the piece of tin on his chest, 'and I hear yuh started a fight in the saloon last night.'

'You heard wrong,' Dace informed

71

him. 'I *prevented* a fight in the saloon last night.'

'I seen Top Perry this morning,' Lawry retorted, as if to put substance in his report. 'Yuh done busted his nose.'

'He came in spoiling for a fight with some gent at my gaming table,' Dace told him. 'I don't win at cards all that often, so I didn't want him ruining my string of luck.'

'Top said yuh kicked him in the knee.'

'Man's twice my size.'

'And yuh hit him in the throat — like to have kilt him for lack of air!'

Dace didn't deny that either. 'If I had hit him hard enough, I reckon it could have killed him.'

'Yuh broke his nose too!'

'I had to convince him not to start a brawl that would break up our game.'

'I could lock yuh up for disturbing the peace.'

Dace studied the man for a moment. 'Were you elected to the office of sheriff?'

The question caught Lawry by surprise. 'Elected?'

'If you weren't elected, who authorized the star you're wearing?'

'Grover Mackenzie gave me the badge,' Lawry answered. 'He's the richest, most powerful man in this part of the country!'

'Enough money can often buy the law, but being rich doesn't give a man the right to appoint the law.'

'Meaning what?'

'I played cards with your town mayor last night . . . Jason Dower,' Dace said. 'Seems to me only a judge or mayor has the power to appoint a sheriff. Did Dower sign off on you being the law in town?'

Lawry threw his hands up in frustration. 'I don't 'member Dower saying squat one way or t'other. What the hell difference does it make who appointed me t' this here job?'

Dace laughed without mirth. 'It matters as to whether you have any real authority or are only a hand-picked stooge for Mackenzie.'

'I ain't no stooge!' The sheriff glowered at Dace — his hands dropped to rest on the butts of his guns. 'Mayhaps I'll have to use gun law t' take you in.'

Dace didn't flinch. 'Be a sorry end if you were to die trying to take a man into custody whose only crime was to stop a fight.'

'What makes you think you could best me with a gun?'

'Common sense,' Dace replied. 'How many men have you drawn down on and killed in a fair fight?'

A grim realization entered the sheriff's eyes. 'I ain't never been in an actual shootout.'

'My point exactly, Sheriff. Besides which, I've nothing to lose — you have your life.'

'You're telling me yuh don't care if yuh live or die?'

'Everything I loved in the world died during the Echo County War. If I had been worried about my life I would

74

have never run down the entire Tanner gang.'

'I see your point,' Lawry admitted. 'Man with nothing t' live for is always more deadly than the man who wants t' keep on breathing.'

'Right you are, Sheriff,' Dace said. 'I'm not the sort of man to be pushed.'

'Yeah.' Lawry puffed up his chest. 'Well, neither am I.'

'It seems we understand one another. Was there anything else you wanted to speak to me about?'

'No, that's it.' Lawry had recovered his composure. 'Don't be starting any more fights.'

'I'll try my best to avoid trouble.'

'Sure yuh will.' Lawry grunted sarcastically, spun about and walked away.

Professor was coming up the street and passed by the lawman. 'Good afternoon, Sheriff!' he chirped the greeting.

'Go squat on a cactus!' Lawry growled back.

The remark caused Professor to frown . . . first at the sheriff and then at Dace. As he drew closer, the expression changed to one of understanding.

'You seem to have wasted little time alienating us from the local constable.'

'Mackenzie gave him his star.'

'He also employs the sizeable lout you dispatched last night.'

'Mackenzie throws a wide loop for a rancher. From listening to the chatter last night, it sounds as if he and his gunmen have cowed most every man in town, including the mayor.'

'The mayor, he owns the mercantile does he not?'

'He does.'

'I have not met him as yet, but I've not been shirking my duties in the snooping department,' Professor told him. 'I learned there are several bullies on Mackenzie's payroll and three hired hands who mostly loiter about at the saloon. If rumors are to be believed, they may well be involved in the theft of cattle from the Greer Ranch.'

Dace reached up to rub his freshly shaven chin. 'Gathering information is good but, with us frozen out by Mrs Greer, I don't see how I can fulfil the deal with Warden Hayward.'

'I may have a solution to that dilemma,' Professor said. Dace paused, allowing him to continue. 'I will assume the role of emissary and ride out to the ranch alone and speak to the Greers. I have some information which the lady may find interesting. Besides which, after a night to ponder her hasty judgement, she might be more receptive to our offer to help.'

'She didn't show any doubt last night.'

'Yes, but she and the young man have had time to discuss our intervention and he may have swayed her thinking somewhat. We ought to provide them with a second opportunity to accept our assistance.'

'You're welcome to try. I won a few dollars playing cards so we've got enough money for another day or two.'

'I shall ride out there forthwith and create a dialogue with the woman. With a measure of good fortune, I'll dissuade her opposition.'

'You do that, Professor.'

Professor whirled about and started off for the livery. Dace watched him go and wondered about the man's dogged determination to stick with someone he had known only as a fellow convict. He said he had other information for Mrs Greer, but Dace hadn't asked what it was. Perhaps he had come up with an angle for the story he wished to write and thought the lady would go along. If his idea resulted in Dace being involved in a shooting war, Professor would have his tale, whether the lady capitulated or Dace even survived.

5

Grover stood at the jail window, with his back to Chuck, looking out to the street. He saw the man who had arrived with Dace Kelly ride past on his way out of town. He wondered if he was leaving, or if he intended to visit the Greer ranch. He mentioned the matter to the sheriff.

'That Bernard Perkins fellow is a writer,' Chuck told him, speaking to his back. 'He bought some notepads and such at Dower's place this morning and asked if we had a local newspaper. Didn't sound like he's intending to leave anytime soon.'

'The question remains, what brings those two men to Tolerance?' Grover wondered aloud. 'They specifically asked if they had reached the Greer ranch when they arrived yesterday.'

'If that's true, it's odd they didn't

stay for a visit out there. Instead, they done rented one of the rooms over at Bo's place.'

'It is a curious situation, Chuck. Seems I remember someone saying Suzanne's older brother is the warden over at Canyon City. Maybe he gave them a message to deliver or something.'

Chuck puckered up as if thinking hard. 'Reckon that could be good news or bad, if her brother sent the two of them here. What do you think?'

'I don't like the idea of having a man like Dace Kelly hanging around town. However, he did say something about needing a job last night. If Suzanne's brother sent him here to work for her, then it's as you pointed out, they would have stayed out at her ranch. As they came to town instead, it means she didn't offer them jobs.'

'I'm not crazy about having someone like him around town,' Chuck said. 'I don't read that guy as being anything but trouble.'

'Have you seen my trio of lazy cowpunchers in town?' Grover asked.

'Bronco is over at the livery getting new shoes on his steed. I 'spect Leets and Cooler ain't out of bed yet. They were still at the saloon when our game broke up sometime after midnight.'

'You weren't there when Perry and Kelly mixed it up?'

'Happened shortly before I arrived. Sounds like Kelly spun him about like a toy top.' He grinned. 'Don't think I'll make the comparison when Topper is around to hear.'

'Not unless you want to be fitted for wooden teeth.'

Chuck returned to business. 'Yuh want me t' tell your boys you're looking for them?'

'I'll speak to them later,' Grover dismissed his offer. 'Any idea how many cattle the Greer ranch is sending to market?'

'I haven't spoken t' Guido or any of the other Lopez boys lately, but I told you they claim to have lost a good many prime beef t' rustlers.'

'Four men to watch that massive ranch,' Grover said, his face a mask of innocence. 'It's a wonder they have any cattle left at all.'

'Yuh got that right, Mac.'

'Tell Smoker I'd like him to keep an eye on our new friend,' Grover told Chuck. 'Kelly's a gunman, just released from prison. If he gets into any more mischief we'll want to know about it.'

'I kin keep an eye on him.'

'You've other responsibilities, Sheriff. Smoker is free to follow Kelly for a day or two.'

'Appreciate the help, Mac. I'll tell him for yuh.'

Grover waved the man out of the sheriff's office and stared off into space. Absently, he reached up and fingered the scratches on the side of his cheek. What a stupid thing to do! Suzanne had no call to claw him like some wildcat. He had been trying to reason with her. Why couldn't she behave in a civilized manner? Her attacking him had caused him to retaliate without thinking. He had struck her with the back of his hand — a purely instinctive reprisal, yet it would be a major sore spot between them for weeks to come.

I ought to ride out and apologize, he thought. *Soothe her concerns during the day and steal her cattle tonight.*

But he knew a woman's ire needed a cooling-down period. His mother had been that way. She would beat him for some small infraction and remain angry for two or three days. Backwards the way that worked. She beat him, but it was *she* who remained irate. She never beat his two sisters, not that he remembered anyway. They were smart enough to both leave home early, each getting married young. His father had been no help, often carrying a scrape or bruise from being hit by anything his ma found handy. Damn, but she was a vicious hot-head sometimes!

The memory caused an uncomfortable churning inside. Being abused had taught him a lesson: he didn't ever want that in his life again. If he had married and had children, he would have been strict, as it was his personality to have his own way, but he would never strike a woman or child in anger. Suzanne had attacked him and his reaction had been automatic, before he had time to think.

Grover thought of his last entry in his accounting journal: it was depressing. No matter how he added up the figures the results were the same. He was nearly bankrupt. He had manipulated nearly everyone in town to gain control over the valley, but the money had run out. He told Chuck they needed to break the Greers before spring, but his business life was on the line too. He had borrowed to his limit from the bank and spent every dime in an effort to acquire Miller's Gap. He was several months behind in his payments and had managed a final extension only until the upcoming cattle drive. He had nearly 200 head ready for the sale, but the prices were not as good this year, because too many herds were moving up from Texas and New Mexico.

He pounded his fist into the palm of his hand. He needed Miller's Gap! It was the only thing that would save him. Money for a toll would provide needed funds to pay his hired hands and return his ranch to solvency. Another few head of cattle would not be enough. No matter what the risk, he had to gain control of the Greer ranch . . . and he needed to do it quickly!

★ ★ ★

Three years of continually living in a place where someone might come up behind a man and pound him silly instilled a sense of awareness in a person. Dace felt eyes on him for several hours before he stopped in front of a store window and caught the phantom's reflection in the glass. It was the man called Smoker, lurking in the shadows, his eyes fixed on Dace's back.

Annoyed at the idea of being

watched, Dace wandered away from the shop window and turned down an alleyway. As soon as he was out of Smoker's sight, he sprinted to the rear of the building and ducked behind the back wall. The wait was not a long one.

Dace heard the man's steps, a bit uncertain at first, wondering where Dace had gone. Then there came the noise of him running next to the building, likely trying to stay hidden in the afternoon shadows. He suddenly appeared and Dace swung his arm like a short pole, catching him under the chin.

Smoker's feet were still moving fast, but his upper body stopped like a calf hitting the end of a lasso — he landed flat on his back, grunting from both pain and surprise. Before he could regain his faculties, he discovered a pistol pointed at him mere inches from his left eye.

'What's the big hurry, Smoker?' Dace asked him icily. 'Why are you following me?'

Smoker's mouth moved but nothing came out. He gulped down a breath and made a second attempt.

'I was heading for an outhouse,' he squeaked breathlessly. 'You know how it is sometimes.'

'The truth, Smoker! You've been a shadow to me all day long.'

'I don't know what you're talking about, Kelly.'

Dace cocked the pistol. 'If there's anything I hate it's someone lying . . . especially to my face. Say hello to the Devil when your soul gets to hell.'

'Wait a minute!' Smoker threw up his hands, one to either side of his face. His eyes crossed as he stared intently at the deadly gun muzzle. 'I'm supposed to keep an eye on newcomers.' He spoke more rapidly than before. 'You know how it is, we don't want any trouble-makers around town . . . and you fit the bill.'

'I do, huh?'

'You warned off my boss last night, then beat the hell out of Top Perry.

Chuck said you practically challenged him to a gunfight . . . and he's the sheriff! You sure ain't been shy about getting into trouble since you arrived.'

'Why the name Smoker?' Dace asked, discharging his claims. 'I don't see the makings for a cigarette in your shirt pockets, no cigars either, and I can't picture you with a pipe sticking out from between your teeth.'

'I picked up the name after some trouble back a few years.'

Dace waited. 'I'm listening.'

'One of the guys who saw me down a gent in a shootout said I had sure smoked him. Another mentioned how I had smoked another fella a few days before. Next thing I knew they were calling me Smoker.'

'And you enjoyed the nickname,' Dace commented.

'Sounds better than Percival Lee Flowers,' he replied.

Dace grinned. 'I can see where that would be a sorry handle for a hardcase tough like you.'

'Look, you want me off of your back . . . I'm gone!' Smoker said with some passion. 'I don't get paid enough to risk my neck over something as tame as watching you shop at the store windows.'

'Why is Mackenzie so worried about newcomers?'

'He's the bull of the valley,' Smoker replied. 'When you're the number one man you always have to watch out for someone who might be number two and looking to move up.'

'Why are you trying to take the ranch away from Mrs Greer and her boy?'

Smoker hesitated, as if he didn't want to give up any more information. Dace planted his boot heel on the man's stomach and applied a fair amount of weight.

'OK, OK!' Smoker gave in at once. 'The boss wants control of Miller's Gap. A person could get rich charging a toll for using the pass. The Greers, like Miller before them, don't believe in charging for access.'

'What about old man Greer? Was that accident arranged by Mackenzie?' Dace suggested.

'I don't know nothing about that, I only follow orders. If I was told to kill a man I'd make him grab for a gun.' He narrowed his gaze at Dace. 'From your reputation, you know all about that kind of killing.'

Dace removed his foot and stepped back. He had learned as much as he was going to from Smoker. 'I don't want you dogging my trail again,' he warned. 'Next time I'll put a bullet in your eye.'

Smoker held up both hands, a sign of surrender. 'If you shoot someone following you, it won't be me. I'm done sneaking around. Time comes for me and you to have a go it'll be man to man.' His face contorted into a sneer. 'And that's something I'll be looking forward to.'

Dace gave an affirmative nod of his head and went around the corner of the building. He moved quickly enough so that Smoker couldn't jump up and shoot him in the back.

The lady might not want me involved in her fight, he thought, *but I seem to be in hot water more than the only bar of soap at a bath house!*

6

Professor rode into the yard at the Greer Ranch expecting to be greeted with a rifle aimed his direction. He was pleasantly surprised when Mrs Greer stepped out and offered him a pleasant smile and a wave.

'I've just taken some hot rolls from the oven,' she said. 'You're welcome to step inside and try a couple.'

'Madam, you are an angel of mercy!' Professor exclaimed. 'I haven't had any fresh bread in nearly two years.'

She didn't speak again, as he climbed down and tied his mount to the hitch rail. He left enough lead rope so the horse could reach the watering trough and then quickly followed the lady into the house.

The heavenly scent from her baking filled his nostrils as he closed the door behind him. He spied the youngster he had seen the previous night sitting at a desk. Nathan — he recalled his name — had a pillow propped up for back support and he looked up from a ledger he had been working on to offer a smile.

'I'm afraid I missed your name last night,' Nathan admitted candidly. 'Once I heard Dace Kelly was your riding partner, I kind of overlooked everything else.'

Professor chuckled. 'He does incorporate a measure of notoriety.' Then he introduced himself for the second time to Nathan and moved over to shake his hand. He paused to admire how the room was neat and tidy. The lady was obviously a fussy housekeeper.

'You were wise to come alone,' Nathan said. 'Sue would have been reaching for the rifle if Dace had been with you.'

'I surmised the welcome might be somewhat chilly after our reception last evening.'

'We have some honey, if you could like some on your rolls?' Mrs Greer spoke from the kitchen.

'Yes, please,' Professor responded, whirling about to continue into the next room. 'May I say again how delightful it is to partake of fresh rolls like a civilized person.'

She smiled politely and set a plate on the table. There were two large, perfect looking rolls next to a small dish of honey.

Professor opened one of the steaming hot rolls and slathered on a substantial amount of honey. As he tasted the first bite, he heaved a sigh of contentment.

'Delicious, my dear lady,' he said between chewing, 'absolutely scrumptious.'

Mrs Greer had two other rolls on a plate and left the room long enough to take them in for Nathan. When she returned, she sat down in the chair opposite Professor and studied him for a long moment.

'All right,' she said, satisfied she knew his purpose for being there. 'Make your sales pitch.'

Professor laughed. 'You are as shrewd as you are a good cook.'

'I won't change my mind about having a gunman in my house.'

After swallowing another mouthful of roll, Professor came to the point. 'We are confronted with an imbroglio, madam. I would not presume to dissuade your stance concerning men who use guns for violence and power. From the opposite perspective, Mr Kelly agreed upon a task in exchange for his early release from prison.'

The woman frowned at the news. 'Bill exhorted Mr Kelly into coming here?'

'He had some concern that you were being forced off of your land. I assure you he seemed genuinely worried for your safety.'

'And upon your arrival you saw me helpless against Grover and his hired man.'

He accepted her statement without rebuttal. 'I spent the latter part of last night and this morning chatting with some local residents. Once I convinced them I was in Tolerance on your behalf, they spoke quite freely about Mr Mackenzie and his men. It would appear the man wishes to own the entire valley.'

'He wants Miller's Gap!' Nathan spoke from the next room. 'The filthy snake will do anything to gain control of the pass.'

'One gentleman was kind enough to point out some rather tough-looking characters, men he described as thieves and rustlers. It took little gleaning of information to confirm Mr Mackenzie has a number of disreputable men on his payroll. The odds seem to be heavily stacked in his favour.'

'I won't stoop to hiring a gunman,' Mrs Greer vowed. 'They are men without honor or conscience; men who kill innocent women and children without a second thought. It was such men who killed my mother.'

'Actually, it is because of your mother that I accompanied Dace.'

'What are you talking about?'

Professor sighed. 'Your maiden name is Hayward! Shelia Heyward was your mother.'

Curiosity transfused to surprise on the woman's face. 'You knew my mother?'

'As I indicated, it is the reason I journeyed here.'

'I don't understand. What do you know about her?'

'Mrs Greer, I — '

'Call me Suzanne,' she interrupted. 'And kindly explain the purpose of your visit.'

'I was attempting to secure a job with a Denver newspaper when I happened onto the story about how your mother was killed during a robbery. I ventured over to nearby Golden to look into the crime and, upon uncovering details of the heinous incident, I came to suspect she was the third victim of a conspiracy.'

'The third victim?'

Professor stared at her intently. 'I

would venture you don't know the real reason your mother was murdered.'

'Real reason?' Suzanne was stunned. 'She was on her way to the general store when she was killed. She was an innocent bystander — shot down in cold blood by one of the three bloodthirsty animals as they made their getaway.'

'Such was the story carried by the local newspaper,' Professor admitted. 'And, truthfully, there is no one to corroborate my different findings, now that Mrs Ellis is dead.'

'You're not making any sense.'

'I believe your mother overheard some ranting during the robbery,' Professor explained. 'Those three men killed her so she would not pass information to the local authorities.' He gave his shoulders a shrug, a sign of helplessness. 'Sadly, all I have is unsubstantiated supposition. I was unearthing facts concerning the shaky partnership between Mr Ellis and his deceased partner, Cal Lawrence, when

I ran afoul of the law and landed in prison.'

Suzanne continued her puzzled look, so he hurried to tell her what little he knew.

'It seems Ellis and Cal had several heated debates over money. Ellis had used profits from the saloon to finance his campaign for mayor. According to the mayor's wife, Cal discovered the monetary losses and demanded Ellis pay back every cent. Shortly after his final demand, the saloon was robbed and Cal was killed, along with the only witness in the room.'

'Yes, the bartender was also shot and killed.'

Professor sighed. 'I suspect those three men must have said something, perhaps even taunted Cal before they killed him. When they spied your mother passing by, they feared she had heard the exchange. They killed her in order to silence her.'

'Mayor Ellis hired those men to kill his partner?'

'Yes, but I lack the means to prove it. Mrs Ellis and I were at a meeting place, where I hoped to coerce more information when' — he cleared his throat — 'uh, we were interrupted. I accidentally started a fire during my escape and wound up serving eighteen months in prison for burning down the local schoolhouse. During my time of incarceration, Mrs Ellis supposedly committed suicide.'

'So you have no proof of your theory?'

'None whatsoever; unless one of the three gunmen comes forward to confess. I admit there is little chance of that happening.'

'No, I suppose not.' Suzanne stared off into space. 'Murder,' she said softly, 'it was murder to keep her from talking.'

'It is difficult to garner information on a case several years old. I believe Mrs Ellis was relating the story to me out of fear for her life.' He paused, agonizing over her death. 'And I let her down.'

'You think the mayor killed her.'

It was a statement, but Professor gave an affirmative nod. 'Her death was listed in the newspaper as a suicide, but I'm certain she would not have taken her own life. She was trapped in a loveless, abusive marriage, but she still harbored optimism and desire for the future.'

'You seem to have gotten to know her pretty well.'

Professor nearly choked on his next swallow, but recovered quickly. 'Yes, enough to know she was telling me the truth.' He blinked to stop his eyes from watering and asked, 'I don't suppose you know of any other witnesses?'

'The town barber heard someone yell a name. One of the three men called out *Let's go, Spider!* That's as much as anyone heard or saw.'

'A soubriquet no doubt.'

'Yes, not much to go on when trying to track down three killers.'

'Tell me, dear lady, what would you do if you knew the identities of the three men responsible for the death of your mother?'

'I would inform the US marshal.'

'What if there was no proof of your claim? What if the law could do nothing to provide the justice such a dreadful deed demands?'

Suzanne put a stern look on Professor. 'I know what you are trying to do,' she said tightly. 'You want me to vindicate the actions taken by your killer friend!'

Professor did not flinch. 'He faced the aforementioned situation. No law, no one willing to testify even if there had there been an inquiry. Everyone who stood or spoke out against the Tanner brothers was terrorized or killed.'

'So your friend was being noble.'

He ignored her sarcasm. 'When the lawless go unpunished, Suzanne, all people suffer the consequences. Dace Kelly resorted to a good man's basic instinct — extinguish the lamp of the wicked.'

'He murdered seven men.'

'No, madam,' Professor corrected, 'he killed seven men in five different duels to the death. His final victory was against the last two Tanner brothers and he had to face them together. He was struck three times by return fire, yet he ended their reign of terror.'

'Dace Kelly was wounded?'

'Not severely, which some might consider as testament that right was on his side.'

To her credit, Suzanne gave a measure of consideration to what Professor had told her. In the end she did not waver.

'I'm sorry,' she said softly. 'I refuse to hire a gunman who would escalate the conflict between Grover and us into a killing war.'

'I applaud your steadfast convictions, madam, though I fear you will suffer defeat because of those very beliefs.'

'I'm glad you stopped by,' she replied. 'I do appreciate you telling me about my mother's death, but I see little hope of ever convicting her murderer.'

'Yes, I had hoped you might shed more light on the circumstances, but it seems we are both to suffer it as a tale without a satisfactory ending.'

'So it would seem . . . Professor.'

He smiled at the informal nickname and rose up from his chair. 'Again, let me express my gratitude for the exceptional dinner rolls, Suzanne. They were an enchantment to the senses.'

'You are very welcome.'

With a short bow, Professor left the kitchen. He waved and said farewell to Nathan as he passed through the sitting-room. Replacing his hat, he stepped out on to the porch —

The jolt knocked him backwards even before the sound of a rifle being fired echoed through the stillness. Professor staggered a step and fell to the floor, stunned from the unexpected blow. His mind raced to catch up. There was a sudden pain as if a red hot branding iron had been driven through his chest.

In a single lucid moment, before the darkness swept over his consciousness, came the terrible realization: *I've been shot!*

* * *

Dace was wondering whether he should give Professor a little more time to return or if he should go ahead and eat when he spied Guido. The man was digging spurs with every bound of his horse, racing along the street. The man spotted Dace and whirled his lathered horse in his direction.

'I'm glad I found you, Kelly,' he said, jerking his mount to a halt and jumping down. 'Your pal has been shot!'

'Professor?' Dace asked, knowing it had to be the case. 'Someone shot him?'

'He was just leaving the ranch and bang! He was hit before he made it out the front door of the house.'

'How is he?' Dace wanted to know.

'Not good. I've come to fetch Jason

— the mayor used to be a medic back during the war.'

'He's at his store,' Dace told him. 'I passed by there not five minutes back.'

Guido waved his thanks and hurried toward the general store. Dace didn't linger, immediately heading for the livery. Bo was mending a wagon spring when he arrived. Before he could finish saddling his horse, the friendly gent moved over to stand at his side.

'Something you might want to know,' Bo said in a hushed voice.

Dace was in a hurry, but he paused long enough to look at him. 'What's that?'

'Those three saddle tramps who sometimes work for Mackenzie were around collecting their horses earlier. They were packing lariats, full saddle-bags, and each had a fish and blankets for bedrolls. I'd wager they were headed out to haze a few head of stray cattle . . . if you know the kind of stray cattle I mean.'

Dace knew a 'fish' was a slang term

for an oilskin rain slicker, and if those boys were riding with ropes attached to their saddles . . .

'They're going to rustle some of Greer's cattle,' Dace deduced.

'I ain't the sort to mistake skunks for house cats, sonny. It would be my guess.'

'Someone ambushed Professor,' he informed Bo. 'Guido came to get the mayor.'

'Dower has tended to a few injuries before,' Bo allowed, immediately showing concern. 'Don't know if I'd want him prodding me with a sharp knife for a bullet, but I 'spect he's as good as we got around here.'

'Thanks for the information on those three men. I'll see if I can maybe ruin their plans if they head for the Greer side of the valley.'

Bo straightened up and regarded Dace with a puzzled look. 'Don't have any idea what you're talking about, Kelly . . . and that's the truth of it.'

'My mistake, I just remembered that

I don't recall who gave me that piece of information.'

'I hope your riding pal is OK,' Bo offered. 'The man talked like he was choosing words by the pound and wanted his money's worth, but I still liked him.'

'I'll let you know as soon as I get back.'

'Good luck.'

Dace swung aboard and put his horse into a ground-covering lope. The ride was much quicker in daylight than when they had come to town from the Greer Ranch. It took only a few minutes before he spied the outbuildings and barn.

Nathan was on the porch when Dace rode into the yard. He took a clumsy first step, regained his balance, and limped forward to meet him.

'Figured you'd be the first to arrive,' he said in greeting. 'It looks pretty bad — bullet went all the way through him and hit the kitchen counter. Lucky Sue wasn't standing in its path.'

'Is Professor conscious?'

Nathan sighed. 'No, he went down hard. He muttered once or twice, but he is pretty much out of this world.'

'You see anything at all?'

Nathan pointed to a patch of scrub oak some sixty paces away. 'The dirty bushwhacker was hiding behind that stand of brush over there. Soon as I heard the shot, I hurried to get to the window. I seen the guy light out on horseback as if his pants were afire.'

'Guido and the mayor should be about ten minutes behind me. I'm going after the shooter.'

'Reckon you haven't forgotten how to track down a killer,' Nathan said meaningfully.

'Your herd is likely to have company tonight,' Dace warned him. 'Three men left town this afternoon, carrying supplies and ropes. You had best be on the lookout for rustlers.'

'I'll have Guido round up the other Lopez boys,' Nathan vowed. 'We have been moving the cattle to a dead-end canyon for roundup. We'll make sure those filthy snakes have to go past us to reach our herd.'

'I'd lend a hand, but I don't want the ambusher's trail to get cold.'

'You've been a real help already, Kelly,' Nathan told him. 'Don't you worry about us or your pal. We'll do everything we can for Bernard, and knowing about the raid, we'll be ready for them too. We really owe you a debt of thanks.'

Dace gave a forward tip of his head. 'I'll be back as soon as I can.'

'Be careful you don't become a second victim!' Nathan called out, as Dace turned his horse around and headed for the brushy area where the shooter had waited.

It didn't take a trained tracker to spot the ambusher's trail. He had mounted his horse after taking the shot and was moving fast, heading away from Tolerance.

During the weeks Dace had run down members of the Tanner brothers and their gang, he had gained consider-able insight in the art of tracking. His first impression told him this shooter was not an experienced killer. He had not bothered to conceal his horse, preferring a quick getaway to stealth. And now he was using the middle of the main road for his escape route. One possibility was he expected no immediate pursuit, or perhaps he intended to mix in his tracks and circle back to Tolerance. After riding several miles, Dace re-evaluated his prey. This guy had no plan. He was as green at ambushing someone as a couple of six-year-olds playing *good guys versus the bad guys.*

* * *

Nathan showed Dower into the house but told Guido to wait at the porch. Once the mayor was tending to the injured man, Nathan returned to talk to his foreman.

'I've received word there may be an

attempt to rustle some of our cattle tonight,' he said, unable to suppress a sense of urgency. 'I know you and your cousins were not hired to do any fighting, but this — '

'We ride for the brand,' Guido interrupted, displaying a grim determination. 'We've lost a couple hundred head in the past two years, because we never had enough men to watch such a large herd. No one is going to take any cattle from us tonight, not while we've got them bunched in Buffalo Canyon.'

'There will be at least three of them,' Nathan went on.

'And there are four of us,' Guido replied. 'Don't worry, Nate, we won't let you down.'

Nathan stuck out his good hand. 'You're worth twice what we can afford to pay you, Guido.'

The man smiled. 'Probably three times as much,' he joked, 'but who wants to work for just the money?' Serious once more, 'There's not a ranch around who would have made me their foreman with my limited experience. You and the lady gave me the job when Eldon died; I aim to prove you didn't make a mistake.'

'Thanks, Guido. Anything you need, you only have to ask.'

'We'll handle it, Nate. You can count on us.'

Nathan watched his hired man climb aboard his horse and head for the box canyon. He felt pride in knowing they had four good men on their payroll. If there were no more than three rustlers, his crew would drive them off. They might even sting their hides enough to make them think twice about trying it a second time.

'Where is Guido off to?' Suzanne asked, having come up behind him in time to see their foreman leaving the yard.

'There's going to be a raid on the herd tonight. Guido is going to have the boys ready to send the would-be rustlers running for cover.'

She moved up beside him. 'Rustlers?

Coming after the herd tonight? When did you learn about this?'

Nathan sighed. 'Dace Kelly was here a few minutes ago. He told me we better be prepared for a raid.'

'But how would he — ?'

'Because he's Dace Kelly!' Nathan answered more bluntly than he intended. Seeing Suzanne's dark expression, he immediately regretted the tone.

'Look,' he hurried to get past the awkward moment, 'Dace arrived ahead of the mayor and Guido. He asked about Professor — I suppose you know he calls Bernard *Professor* — and then he told me he suspected three men were likely going to attack the herd tonight. I told him Bernard was unconscious and didn't look too good.'

'So he left without seeing him?'

'He isn't welcome on our property, remember?'

The tight little frown returned. 'I wouldn't have stopped him from seeing his wounded friend. I'm not that cold and vindictive.'

'Well, it didn't matter one way or the other, Sue. Soon as I told him Bernard was unconscious and pointed out where the ambusher had fired from, he took off to follow his trail.' Nathan could not help allowing himself a smug remark. 'There's one murdering coyote who won't get away without paying his due. Kelly will see to that.'

Suzanne did not comment on Kelly. 'Do you think Guido and the Lopez brothers can handle the rustlers?'

'Yes,' Nathan again showed confidence, 'the rustlers will have to try and enter the box canyon. The trail narrows through the mouth enough that the boys can easily set up an ambush and be ready for them. Those three raiders are going to be in for a real surprise.'

Suzanne wrung her hands. 'I hope none of our men gets hurt.'

Nathan turned to face her. 'They are all good hands, Sue. When a man hires on to help run a cattle spread he expects to have to fight on occasion, whether it be against the weather,

Indians or rustlers. Guido said he and the others rode for the brand. In plain English, that means they will defend the ranch and our cattle!'

'You took it upon yourself to give orders,' she said, displaying an odd sort of pride. 'I guess it's time I accepted that you are becoming a man.'

'I know I'm young and not a full-sized yet,' Nathan replied, feeling about a foot taller, 'but I'm working on it.'

Suzanne reached out, took hold of his arm and smiled. 'You're going to be there before you know it.'

7

Dace topped a slight rise and stopped, allowing his animal to blow. He had chosen a good horse, possessing a mix of speed and endurance, yet an easy ride. Rising to stand in the stirrups, he could make out a distant speck crossing the open country ahead. He had to wonder where the man was going . . . certainly not back to Tolerance. Pausing to look skyward, he had maybe two hours of daylight left. If the man stopped to camp, it would be his last mistake. There would be a full moon and the trail was the same one he and Professor had used on their ride into the valley.

'Bet you didn't expect anyone to dog your trail so soon,' Dace said aloud. 'Well, my bushwhacking friend, I'm going to run you to ground.'

Even as he spoke he was curious.

Had the attacker intended to shoot Professor, or had he thought Dace would be the one coming out the front door? Did he even know who he had shot? Perhaps he was there to intimidate Mrs Greer and young Nathan. Shooting anyone in the doorway would have been a dire warning. With rustling scheduled for tonight and shooting someone at the house, it would have been a double blow.

Pondering over the possibilities he decided an unwarranted attack during the day would be more likely to put the Greer people on alert — the exact opposite of what the night raiders would have wanted. Better strategy to catch the ranch hands asleep or unwary. Shooting someone from ambush would raise the alarm and make it more of a risk to try and rustle any cattle.

Plus the rider was heading away from Tolerance. If he was in league with Mackenzie he would have swung wide, gone off into the hills and tried to hide his trail. Eventually, he would have returned to town or the ranch on the other side of the valley. His direction of flight made no sense.

Involved once more in a manhunt brought back clandestine memories, dark days of riding, hunting, challenging and killing members of a murderous band of cutthroats. Dace had been raised by God-fearing parents and knew right from wrong. He justified his actions as being necessary to stop future murders and raids. Without proper law, it was the responsibility of just men to punish the criminals lest chaos rule the land. Had he tried, he might have been able to gather a posse together before going after the Tanner brothers — he chose to do it alone. Perhaps that was the difference upon which Judge Roper had based his determination. Justice would have been the order of men, not the punishment dispensed by a single man. Dace understood why Roper termed his actions as vengeance rather than justice. Dismissing his misgivings or further moral debate, he put his horse into an easy lope and kept the speck within sight.

★   ★   ★

Suzanne was a few feet away when Professor came awake with a start. He groaned from the sudden movement and his eyes opened wide in surprise.

'I . . . I'm not dead?' he said aloud, as if altogether uncertain.

Suzanne stepped over to the bedside. 'You're stuck here on earth with the rest of us mortals, Professor. The mayor cleaned the wound and bandaged the two holes in your body. He said it was a miracle the bullet missed your lung and heart.'

Professor rotated his head so he could look at her. 'I should like to claim the good fortune is due to my spiritual endeavors and clean living, but it would be a falsehood.' He smiled at her. 'It is very hospitable of you to provide me with medical aid and a bed.'

'You were shot leaving our house,' she stated.

'Has Dace been informed of my situation?'

'He's on the trail of the man who shot you,' she informed him. 'If his reputation is deserved, he will undoubtedly avenge the shooting.'

'You speak as if resentful of his actions,' Professor observed.

'More killing won't settle anything.'

'I fear you still misunderstand Dace Kelly.'

'I understand he killed seven men,' she retorted.

Professor grimaced from trying to shift his weight and immediately had second thoughts about that. Relaxing again, he rolled his head back and forth slightly.

'Pardon my bluntness, but you understand nothing, Mrs Greer,' he said quietly, sincerely. 'Dace is not what you think.' He didn't wait for her to argue, but began a story. 'I had been incarcerated at Canyon City for a short few days when a vicious brute attacked me. He would have killed me if Dace had not come to my defense. Dace didn't know me — we had not even spoken to one another — yet he jumped in and knocked the bully down. He did the same thing for your hired man in town. He didn't know Guido worked for you; he stood up for a stranger to save him from a severe beating and possible death.

'You wish to categorize him as a hired killer, a man with a gun and no conscience, but you would be consummately wrong. There were nights in prison and again along the trail, when I was witness to him suffering dreadful nightmares. After a sleepless and fitful night, he related to me how he was troubled by each man's final words, shock or sudden anguish which shone on his face at the moment of death. I relate this to you in confidence, assured you will keep our conversation private. Dace would not want people to know how the killing of those men haunts him every day.'

'Perhaps, but he still managed to kill all of them.'

'Dace worked a small ranch with his father and brother, much the same as you, your husband and Nathan. They were a tightly knit family until his brother met a girl and brought her home to meet his father. Dace was drawn to her at once and he confided to me that she viewed him with favor as well. It was a triangle which could have torn the family apart, so Dace did the honorable thing. He left the valley and moved to Denver. He walked away from a woman he wanted for his own, because his brother loved her.'

Suzanne grew pensive, considering the story, so Professor gave her a few moments before he continued. 'The raiders came to the valley and began attacking farms and ranches, driving people out or killing them. Dace's father and brother, along with his brother's new wife, would not run. They stayed to fight for their home and property.

'One fatal night seven men attacked their ranch and they battled back from inside their house. The place was set afire and it was confirmed by one of Tanner's men how they heard a woman's screams after the roof caved. Those cowardly villains roasted the three of them alive before driving off their stock.' He paused. 'I have been friends with Dace these past eighteen months, yet he didn't tell me the whole truth until we were on our way here. Three years he spent in prison, Suzanne, granite hard, with nerves of steel and the courage of a wolverine, yet his eyes filled with tears of emotion when he told me the tale.'

'What you say might be true, but — '

Professor lifted a hand to prevent her continuing. 'You have done me a great service, treating my wound and allowing me to recover. I would not presume to force either Dace or myself into your life. My purpose in speaking up is so you might more readily understand Dace Kelly. As I told you previously, Dace came here to help and I accompanied him so I could speak to you about your mother.'

'If Mr Kelly returns,' Suzanne spoke softly, as if considering every word, 'I shall allow him the chance to speak his mind . . . before I ask him to leave a second time.'

'I would appreciate your providing that singular courtesy.'

'Reckon it's about time,' Nathan called from the next room.

'All right, Nate,' Suzanne replied. 'Douse the lamps and take up a position at the window. I'll move the cow from the barn and put her on a lead rope where she can feed down by the creek.'

Professor frowned. 'Why all the precautions? Are you expecting more trouble?'

'Dace warned us that three characters from town were headed out to our place,' Nate spoke again. 'He guessed they were going to try and steal cattle, so we have the crew prepared for that. However, we are going to keep watch during the night in case they decide to attack the house or set fire to the barn instead.'

'Sound logic,' Professor approved. 'I wish I could be of some help.'

'You lie back and get some rest,' Suzanne instructed him. 'I don't intend to wait on you hand and foot for a week or two.'

'Of course not,' Professor replied. 'I shall be ready to ride by tomorrow.'

She regarded him with a cynical lift of one eyebrow. 'And I thought Dace was the indestructible man of iron.'

Professor tested his strength and grunted from a sudden spasm of pain. 'Perhaps setting a departure time is a bit premature. I'm not sure I could sit a horse just yet.'

'Go to sleep,' Suzanne told him a second time, 'we'll try not to wake you unless the shooting starts.'

'Very thoughtful of you, madam . . . uh, Suzanne,' Professor replied. 'Very thoughtful indeed.'

* * *

Dace smelled smoke long before he spied the camp. Once he caught a glimpse of the flickering of a campfire, Dace tied off his horse and approached on foot. The bushwhacker was either very confident, or leaving the scene of an ambush was new to him. Moving silently, Dace wove a path through the brush until he could make out the man hunkered next to the fire.

'Sonuva bee!' he growled under his breath. Straightening up, he strode out into the open.

'You're a long way from Canyon City,' he spoke loudly to the prison guard he knew as Granger.

The man scrambled for his rifle as Dace moved to within a few feet of him. He grabbed up the weapon by the time he recognized his visitor. Even in the dim light from the fire, Granger paled noticeably. 'Kelly?'

Dace hadn't drawn his pistol but it was no longer secured by the thong strap. 'Want to tell me about it, Granger?'

'Tell you about what?'

'Don't play dumb, Granger,' Dace warned him. 'You tried to have the professor killed while he was in prison but it didn't work. Now you ride as far as Tolerance to do the job yourself. Why is it so important to get rid of him?'

Granger gave his head a negative shake. 'I don't have a quarrel with you, Kelly.'

Dace bore into him with an icy gaze. 'I haven't got but one friend in the world and you may have killed him — that's the short route to starting a quarrel.'

'I've got my rifle pointed at you, Kelly.' Granger tried to sound menacing, waggling the end of the barrel as a warning.

'And I'm supposed to think you have a round in the chamber, is that it?'

'I can kill you where you stand,' he warned. Then he quickly changed his tone, 'Or we could do this together.'

'Do what together?' Dace asked, curious to discover the truth.

'Five thousand dollars, Kelly,' Granger told him, speaking rapidly. 'I've got a bank draft in my saddle-bags for a thousand and there's four thousand more when the job is done. It would take me five years working at the prison to earn that much money!'

Dace arched his eyebrows at the news. 'Five thousand dollars for killing Bernard Perkins? Someone with a lot of money must have a good reason to want him dead.'

'It's a guy I know over in the Denver area. We were in the war together — the Colorado Volunteers.'

'I remember; the men directly responsible for stopping the Confederate Army from Texas, when they tried to gain control of the goldfields from New Mexico to Colorado back in '62.'

'That's right!' he declared enthusiastically. 'We were with Major Chivington at the battle of La Glorieta Pass. We turned them Johnny Rebs back and saved the war for the Union.'

'So how did a couple heroes from the

war end up as a pair of coyotes?'

Granger's face darkened with anger. 'Ellis and his partner struck it rich up near Leadville. They sold their mine for enough to build a big saloon in Golden.' He shrugged. 'Ellis ran for election and won the job of mayor, but he went in debt to do it. When his partner complained too loudly he ended up the dead victim during a holdup.'

'And Bernard discovered the mayor's involvement,' Dace finished the tale.

'Ellis had a wife who talked too much,' Granger explained.

'And she died of a mysterious suicide some time back.'

Granger shrugged. 'That's how the law declared her death.'

'And this Ellis is paying five thousand dollars to keep Bernard from finishing his investigation.'

'The man wants to sleep at nights.'

'How about you, Granger?' Dace asked. 'How does a cold-blooded bushwhacker sleep at nights?'

'Look, Kelly, I liked Perkins. I had nothing against him. But with this money I'll be . . . *we*,' he corrected quickly, 'we could be set for life!'

'Professor might not be dead. He was alive when I left the Greer ranch.'

'Ellis doesn't have to know that, Kelly,' Granger hurried to convince Dace. 'I was supposed to bring that stupid ring Perkins wears — proof he was dead, that sort of thing. But the ring doesn't matter, Ellis will believe me. We can go to Denver together and get the money. With that much cash we can get a fresh start, buy our own business or whatever!'

'It doesn't take a lot of money to last a man a lifetime,' Dace said, his tone hedged with frost, 'if his life is short enough.'

'I don't want to kill you, Kelly,' Granger said menacingly, 'but I will.'

'If you already had a bullet in the chamber of that rifle, you wouldn't have offered to split the money,' Dace replied easily. 'You're going to stand before

Judge Roper for attempted murder . . . even if Professor lives.'

Granger cocked the rifle with lightning speed, levering a live round into the chamber. He slid his finger to the trigger certain he had caught Dace off guard! A smile flashed to his face as he aligned the barrel at the target. He had him! He was going to be the man who killed Dace Kelly! He would be famous! He would be written up in the penny dreadful magazines! Everyone would know . . .

The single bullet struck a microsecond before the sound of a gunshot. Granger's thought processes came to a screaming halt! He didn't realize his face was flattened against the ground and his open mouth had taken an involuntary bite of dirt. His life had ended with the entry of a small, lead projectile into his brain.

'You got off easy, Granger,' Dace spoke to the corpse. 'Too damned easy.'

★ ★ ★

Grover was up early to see how the evening raid had gone. He spied Smoker at the cafe and wandered over to join him. Before he had even sat down, Smoker shook his head.

'Last night was a bust, Mac,' he said bitterly, 'a fiasco, an utter failure.'

'What happened?'

'They were ready for the boys. Bronco took a bullet in the thigh and Leets was stung in the left arm. They were lucky to escape with their lives.'

Grover gnashed his teeth. 'How could the Greers have known we were going to hit them?'

'I don't know.'

'You think it was a lucky break on their part? Maybe they happened to see our men coming?'

Smoker shrugged. 'Cooler says no way, but I wouldn't trust him not to lie through his teeth. I never liked those three renegades. They are the kind with no loyalty to anyone but themselves.'

'I pay them because they have no ties here, Smoker. They can do a job and disappear if need be. We need them for the time being . . . especially with Dace Kelly in the valley.'

'Kelly warned me to stop following him,' he admitted to Grover. 'Man must have eyes in the back of his head. Stuck a gun in my face and told me he'd kill me next time.'

'What did you say to that?'

'I told him the next time we would see who was the better man with a gun!' Smoker rubbed his jaw. 'Didn't scare him none, but I think he believed me.'

'Perhaps we underestimated Kelly. A man who tracked down seven hardcase killers and put each and every one in their grave has some special skills.'

'You give the word and I'll try him on for size.'

'Not yet,' Grover said. 'I wonder if he somehow got wind of our little raid and warned the Mexicans?'

Smoker frowned in thought. 'Could be he overheard some talk, or spotted the boys leaving town. Either way, the boys didn't fare well in the rustling business last night.

'Did you hear about someone shooting Kelly's pal, the newspaper gent? Story goes he was shot leaving the ranch house.'

'No, you're the first man I've spoken to. What happened? Was the shooter after him or did he think it would be Dace Kelly stepping out the front door?'

'No one knows, Mac. I spoke to Dower and he said the guy would probably pull through all right. Nathan also told Dower that Kelly lit out after the ambusher.'

'Why would anyone want to shoot the news hound?'

Smoker snickered. 'I don't know, but we shouldn't count on ever seeing that *hombre* alive again. If he ain't already dead, he's living his last days. Kelly will run him to ground before he knows someone is on his trail.'

'It's still a mystery why he and the newsman came to the valley. Kelly didn't stay out at the ranch, so it doesn't look as if he's working for Mrs Greer.'

'Maybe not, but the newspaper man went back out there yesterday. One of them must have a reason for visiting.'

'And it's obvious someone warned the Greer cowpokes we were coming.'

Smoker tipped back his hat to scratch his head. 'Nothing makes much sense at the moment, Mac. What's our next move?'

'How badly hit are the two men? Do they need Dower to look at their injuries?'

'Naw, both of them only had flesh wounds. They pretty much bandaged one another up and are looking for some payback.'

Grover waited while being served coffee and a plate of ham and eggs. It gave him a few moments to think, but he was still groping in the dark.

'This whole business is going south and there doesn't seem to be any way to turn it around. Since Kelly arrived we've had a string of bad luck . . . most of it with his help!'

'Yeah, but like you said, Mrs Greer didn't put him or the newsman up at the ranch.' Smoker swore. 'We're in the dark, Mac . . . and I hate the dark!'

'And maybe Perkins went to the ranch to warn them of the raid.'

'I suppose he could have been the one who passed the information about the boys planning to rustle some cattle. Even if he did, it don't explain who shot him or why.'

'It's spilled milk at this point,' Grover complained. 'And I suppose the news jockey will be laid up for a few days, until he can ride as far as town.'

'You want me to take a ride that direction and see what I can find out?'

'It might look like we have a vested interest in this whole affair,' Grover said, considering the possibilities. 'We don't want anyone thinking we had a hand in shooting the newsman from ambush.'

'Then we stay in the dark.'

'We'll wait for Kelly to make the next move.'

'You're the boss,' Smoker said. 'What do I tell the three morons?'

Grover reached into his vest pocket and removed a few bills. 'Give this to them; it'll tide them over for a couple days. Tell them to stay ready. We have to break Suzanne and Nathan before next spring or I'll be the one going bankrupt.'

'I'll tell them they best heal up quick,' Smoker vowed, rising up from the table. He put a few coins by his plate to pay for the meal. 'I'll see you later.'

Grover watched him leave and began to eat. The meal wasn't as good as the food Kendall's wife prepared. With him being the ranch owner, he could have eaten all of his meals with his manager, but Kendall's kids were a nuisance to be around. They were well behaved, but kids were kids. Sniffing at runny noses, whispering back and forth, playing at the table, whining about the food or constantly wanting or needing something . . . they were kids!

He grunted in disgust. *If the world had to rely on me to populate the next generation, the planet would sure enough end up a soulless wasteland!*

8

Rather than return to town, Dace rode to the Greer ranch. He wanted to check on the professor before he did anything else.

Nathan was on the garden side of the house, supporting his weight by leaning on a shovel, while he used a hoe and his good hand to cut some unwanted weeds. He spotted Dace, dropped his tools and hobbled over to the front porch.

'I should have taken the bet with Bernard . . . Professor,' he corrected. 'He said you wouldn't be back until tomorrow.'

Dace stopped his mount and Granger's horse, which he had on a lead rope, and climbed down. 'The professor probably gave the ambusher credit for being somewhat smarter than a bucket of rocks.'

Nathan laughed. 'Then you found him?'

'About thirty miles from here,' Dace answered, while tying off both animals so they could reach the watering trough.

The door swung open and Suzanne Greer appeared. She wore an apron over a drab, grey dress and her hair was pulled back with a royal blue ribbon. She paused to hold up a hand to shade her eyes from the afternoon sun. Her gaze went to the pair of horses.

'The ambusher is dead?'

Dace hated how the question sounded more like an accusation, but answered politely. 'He had no stomach for prison, ma'am — tried to kill me rather than surrender.'

'Like the Tanners, I suppose.'

'No, they were guilty of several murders,' Dace informed her. 'They would have hanged. The reason this guy didn't want to go to jail is because he had been a prison guard . . . working for your brother!'

The news caused her to recoil. 'He

was one of Bill's prison guards?'

'He passed a note to a bully there at the prison, soon after Professor arrived. The idea had been to kill Professor while he was behind bars. When that plan failed, the guard followed us here and tried to finish the job himself.'

Suzanne appeared in deep thought for a moment. Then she tipped her head at the trough. 'You best wash off some of the dust from your ride. Supper is nearly ready.'

Dace put a curious frown on Nathan. The youth displayed a wide smile. 'Guess that means you're staying!'

'How's Professor?'

Nathan waved a dismissive hand. 'He'll be up and poking his nose into other people's business in no time. Dower said the bullet went clean through and didn't damage much more than muscle. He was real lucky.'

Dace felt an immediate relief and headed toward the watering trough. 'I do believe I'm carrying enough trail dust to fill a flour barrel.'

'I've a towel inside,' Nathan offered. 'Time you get washed up, I'll have it ready so you can dry off.'

'I'm obliged.'

Supper turned out to be roast beef, potatoes and corn bread. It was the best meal Dace had tasted since leaving his home. Professor was able to feed himself, but fell asleep almost at once after the effort. When the meal was finished, Nathan made a point of saying he had chores to do and left the house.

'I'm not much of a hand at washing dishes,' Dace confessed, uncomfortable at being alone with a woman, 'but I can sure enough dry them for you.'

She didn't object, so he helped her clear away the table and she heated a pan of water for cleaning. Shortly, Suzanne was washing and passing plates to Dace.

'I'm curious about this man you chased down,' she said after a short time. 'Did he say why he wanted to kill Professor?'

'Seems my snoopy pal learned a dirty

secret about a man who was elected mayor over in Golden — that's a few miles out of Denver. The fellow's name is Ellis and he knew Granger, the prison guard, from back during the war. The two of them had kept in touch, so the mayor knew Granger worked at Canyon City. He contacted him and asked him to take care of Professor. When he didn't get the job done at the prison, he followed him here and tried a second time.'

'I spoke to Professor earlier and he told me he thinks the mayor is responsible for my mother's death.'

Dace nearly dropped a plate. 'Your mother's death?'

'The mayor owns the biggest saloon in Golden. He and his partner built and ran it together. There was a holdup and the mayor's partner was killed . . . along with a bartender and my mother.'

'So Professor came here to see you!' Dace declared. 'It had nothing to do with me.'

Mrs Greer continued with what she

had learned. 'Professor said the mayor's wife told him the robbery was a hoax to cover up the intended murder of his partner. And yes, the reason he tagged along with you was to visit with me and find out what, if anything, I knew.'

'Then Professor is still trying to prove the mayor's involvement.'

'Yes, but he lost what little proof he had when Mrs Ellis died from apparent suicide while he was in prison.'

'He did mention the man's wife to me. He didn't seem to think she would have killed herself.'

Mrs Greer stopped her work and turned to look squarely at Dace. 'Knowing what you do about Granger, if you were to help Professor, could you put Ellis behind bars?'

'Doesn't seem likely with no witnesses. His wife might have provided the proof but she is dead.'

The lady vented her frustration. 'There must be a way, Mr Kelly! That man ordered his partner killed and is responsible for my mother's murder!'

Dace looked at her, eyes bright with fury, a plea on her lips . . . and his mind went blank.

Dang it all! he thought. *Those are the prettiest eyes and most perfect lips I've ever seen!*

'What?' she asked, her brows pulled a bit tighter with wonder. 'What is it?'

'Huh?' Dace responded dumbly.

'You were looking at me like you wanted to say something.'

Dace cleared his throat awkwardly. 'Ma'am, I've been away from female companionship for three years and you're about the most beautiful — ' He stopped in mid-sentence, before making a bigger fool of himself. 'I apologize for staring,' he finished lamely.

The lady turned away, but not before Dace saw a crimson flush rise in her cheeks. Without another word she returned to washing the dishes with a renewed gusto. The pace was so rapid Dace had a hard time keeping up.

Nathan entered the house as the last dish was dried and Suzanne began to put everything away in its proper place. The youth didn't seem to notice the awkward silence, walking into the kitchen and pausing to lean against the wall.

'I put both your horse and the spare mount in the corral for you,' he told Dace. 'The bunkhouse is empty, what with the guys riding a twenty-four hour watch for rustlers. You look plum tuckered out from the ride, so I figure you might as well take advantage of an empty bed.'

'Speaking of rustlers, did those three men show up to raid your cattle last night?'

'They came snooping all right,' Nathan said with some satisfaction. 'The boys sent them wailing down the canyon like three pups with their tails afire. They'll think twice before they try stealing any more of our cattle.'

'Why does Mackenzie want your place so badly?'

'Miller's Gap; it's the only short route through the mountain range for all of the cattlemen and travelers down south. Even the stage uses the trail — saves everyone fifty miles going and coming.'

'And Mackenzie would put a toll on the passage,' Dace reasoned.

'You got it.'

'How are you two holding out?' Dace asked. 'Warden Hayward talked as if you were close to losing the place.'

Before Mrs Greer could speak up Nathan answered. 'We are skirting the edge of a deep canyon, Kelly. If those rustlers had run off even a few head of our cattle, we might not have been able to meet the mortgage payment this year. Truth is, we've sat back and done nothing while Mackenzie has stolen a third of our herd.'

'Any way to prove it?'

'He is quick to alter the brands, so we don't have any leverage to get the cattle back . . . even if we had real law around here. I would guess that's why William thinks we're about to go bankrupt.'

'Nate!' the lady jumped in, showing an immediate displeasure by glaring at

148

him. 'We might have to tighten our belts, but we are not to the point of hiring gunmen and killers!'

Dace flinched at her outburst and decided a retreat was in order. He stepped around the table and picked up his hat. 'Appreciate the use of a room for the night, Nathan,' he thanked the young man. 'I'll check in and see how Professor is before I leave in the morning.' He gave a courtesy nod at the lady. 'And thank you for a very fine meal, ma'am.' Then he walked through the main room and went out the door.

Suzanne groaned inwardly at the hurt look on Nathan's face. Once Dace Kelly was out of earshot she reached out to take hold of his hand.

'I'm sorry, Nate,' she murmured. 'I didn't mean to — '

Nathan jerked away. 'I know!' he snapped at her. 'You judge him the same as those guys who shot your mother.' He whirled about and headed for his room. 'But Dace isn't guilty of anything except dealing out justice!' He limped another few steps before turning to bark at her, 'If you were a man, Sue, you'd have gone after those men who killed your mother and done the same thing!'

Suzanne started to call after him but thought better of it. What could she say . . . that he was right?

* * *

Although bone tired Dace couldn't get to sleep. He had spent an hour in the same room with the most desirable woman he had met since Anne. For the first time in nearly four years, he realized the adage *time heals all wounds* might have some validity. Lying in the dark, he could no longer picture Anne clearly in his mind . . . odd, considering it was all he could think of during his many weeks of tracking down the Tanner gang. And the pain of her death, which had caused him as much grief as the loss of his father and brother, was no longer acute and debilitating.

He had seen something in Mrs Greer's eyes, a complex yearning he didn't understand. It obviously was not intended for him, but he had seen it, a brief glimpse, a single moment when her guard had been down. And the almost pursed lips, as if she was prepared for a lover's kiss . . .

'For hell sakes, Dace!' he growled under his breath. 'Thoughts like those are sure gonna help you get to sleep!'

At that moment the door opened a crack.

Dace scrambled to get his holster, fumbling to locate the thong so he could remove the pistol. If Mackenzie's men had come to kill him, he would take one or more of them with him!

'Mr Kelly?' a feminine voice whispered. 'Are you asleep yet?'

Dace dropped the holster on the bed and pulled the covers up to his chest. 'Uh, not yet,' he stammered inanely.

Without a word of explanation, Mrs Greer put a match to the wall lamp and adjusted the flame to a low setting.

When she looked at him a smile tugged at the corners of her mouth.

'I'm no stranger to a man without a shirt, Mr Kelly. You needn't be afraid of me. I've only come to talk.'

Dace felt outright foolish with the blanket tugged up almost to his chin. Struggling for a minute tad of courage, he tossed the cover aside and swung his legs over the side of the bed. He had removed his shirt because it was on the gamey side, but he still wore his trousers and socks as a precaution.

'You're still dressed?' she asked, taking notice of his attire.

'If raiders attacked to burn you out or something, I wanted to be ready. Being without your trousers is a real disadvantage in most any kind of fight.'

She laughed, the first natural response he had gotten from her.

'Is something wrong?' he queried, baffled at her showing up after everyone had supposedly gone to bed for the night.

She appeared to take a deep breath,

then strode over and sat down on the bed next to him. He enjoyed how she had brushed out her hair, and being so near . . . his heart accelerated, shifting from a natural beat to a thundering sprint.

'I was rude to you this evening,' she began, her voice as soft as a baby's whisper. 'I have never been rude to a guest in my house before. And I hurt Nate's feelings . . . something I haven't done in a long time.'

'You only voiced your opinion,' Dace excused her earlier comment. 'I don't blame you for not wanting a gunfighter or killer around.'

'I was a little girl when my father joined the Union to fight against slavery. He was mortally wounded at Vicksburg. When my mother was killed, I was barely seventeen.' She exhaled, as if she had been holding her breath. 'I came here to tend to Nate because I needed a home and a way to earn my keep. Nate was badly crippled and the doctor who treated him said he might never walk again.

'The first year was filled with long and dreary days. Nate and I often battled about what he could and couldn't do. When we finally came to terms, he began to work his muscles and grow stronger. It took six months before he could take a step without using crutches. That night, we celebrated his achievement with ice cream and cake.

'Eldon Greer loved and cherished his wife. He was a gentle and caring father and treated me like a step-daughter. Grover arrived in the valley and Mr Miller was killed in a hunting accident a few months later. When Eldon learned Mr Miller had left his ranch to us, he became fearful for our safety.' She paused, as if wondering why she was telling this to a perfect stranger. 'In the end, he asked me to marry him so he could protect the ranch. He wanted to preserve it for Nathan.'

'Sounds like a good man,' Dace put in.

'He also knew there was talk about town, due to the fact I was living out here with him and his son without a chaperon. I'm sure Grover was behind most of the gossip, but our marriage put an end to the scandalous rumours.'

'And Eldon's sudden death?'

'I don't think anyone believes he was killed in a wagon mishap. Eldon had been around wagons and teams all his life. He would have never lost control and simply tipped over. Guido rode out to the place where he died and said there were not even any skid marks. The wagon had been turned over . . . probably *after* Eldon was killed.'

'A big, strong man could have broken his neck,' Dace surmised. 'That fellow Perry is big enough to get the job done.'

'Before Eldon was even laid to rest, Grover came calling, offering me support and wanting to buy the ranch or join together in a partnership.'

'Only met him the night I arrived, but he did strike me as the benevolent sort,' Dace said sarcastically.

'Grover knows Eldon and I were never romantically inclined.' As if to answer his unasked question, she added, 'When we said our wedding vows Eldon kissed me on the cheek.'

'I see.'

'The thing is, Mr Kelly, I've had to be strong since the day my mother died. I had to see to her funeral and sell everything we owned to pay the bills she had run up. Before she was murdered, we were both working for a hotel ... cleaning rooms, washing laundry and doing a little of everything. We barely eked out a living between the two of us. I only managed to accept the job here because Eldon sent me travel money and a pass for the stage.

'When I arrived I became housekeeper, cook and older sister all at once. I had to be strong for both Nate and Eldon. When Eldon was killed, I saw to his affairs and communicated back and forth with our bank in Denver. I took over managing the ranch with Nate and Guido to guide me.' Mrs Greer's hands were clasp together on her lap and her chin was tucked to her chest. 'I'm so very tired of being strong and brave.' She murmured the last words again, 'So very tired.'

'I know what you mean,' Dace spoke sympathetically. 'For nearly four years I didn't dare turn my back to anyone, never let my guard down — it might have meant my death. Tracking the murdering maggots who killed my family, then three years watching my own back in prison, it takes a toll on a person.'

'Yes,' she whispered, 'but you're a strong and fearless man.'

'Man or woman, everyone needs someone they can turn to, lean on, feel they don't have to face the world alone.'

'I . . . ' The young woman's voice cracked from emotion. 'I don't know how much longer I can do this . . . be strong for Nate . . . be responsible for . . . '

'You don't have to tackle this battle alone, ma'am,' Dace told her gently. 'If you'll allow me to help, I'll see to it you don't lose the ranch.'

Dace needed quick reflexes. A brawl or gunfight sometimes erupted with no warning. He had sharpened his faculties, honed his alertness, prepared himself for any contingency . . . or so he had thought.

The turning of her body was his only warning — Dace had no time to muster a defence. Suzanne threw her arms around him, dipped her head in beneath his chin and began to sob against his chest.

Dace was more than caught unaware, he was utterly thunderstruck. Of anything he might have expected from the lady, having her break down and cry on his shoulder was two or three rungs below the last step on his ladder of possibilities.

Sanity slowly crept back to his being. Dace recovered wits enough to encircle her in his arms. In an effort to afford some comfort, he began a slow and gentle rock, as if holding an infant. He whispered words of solace and support, anything he could think of. After a few minutes, she ceased weeping, but remained firmly locked within his embrace. They were poised like two dancers who wished to remain entwined yet lacked the strength to stand. Finally, when he thought she must have fallen asleep, the lady stirred. He quickly withdrew his arms so she could sit back.

'I'm sorry,' she said, wiping at her eyes with her fingers, 'I-I don't know what came over me. I've never done anything like that before.'

'Even the strongest of people need to let go of their emotions on occasion.'

'Of course.' She didn't sound convinced.

'For me, it was a *snuggle bear* in my cell,' he said, attempting to lighten the mood. 'I told the guards I wanted to make it for a niece, but it was really for me.'

The suggestion of a grin lifted at the corners of her mouth. 'A snuggle bear?'

'One of the guards liked to whittle. I had him carve a wooden head of a bear cub and then I wrapped some layers of cotton around it for a body and covered it with a dyed-brown flour sack. It doubled as a pillow, except for the head of course. I kept it as my cell mate for three years.'

'How very manly.'

Dace smiled. 'Like I said, everyone needs someone.'

The woman's eyes lifted and she regarded him with a candid gaze. 'You're certainly not like any of Grover's gunmen. Perhaps Nate is right about you being different.'

'I suspect, if I don't think about it too hard, that might be an off-handed compliment.'

'You're compassionate . . . and for-giving,' she went on. 'I was rude to you in the house and yet you comforted me like an injured child. I called you a killer and you said I was beautiful.'

'There's truth in both statements, ma'am.'

'Suzanne,' she corrected.

'So what made you come out here for

a visit, Suzanne?'

She sobered. 'It's something Nate said — yelled would be a better term. He said if I could have, I would have done the same thing you did.'

'You mean go to prison for three years?'

'Kill the men responsible for my mother's death.' She took a deep breath and let it out slowly. 'I like to think of myself as a genteel woman, but I can't deny the urge to find and kill the three ruthless bandits who murdered my mother.'

'Truth is I would have preferred to have had a judge and jury, rather than killing those men myself. Awaiting trial, watching the gallows being built, waiting for the end, knowing you are condemned to an eternity in hell — that would have been a more befitting punishment than a quick death.'

'Did you really have no other choice?'

Dace shrugged. 'If I had managed to capture a couple of them alive and got them to Denver, they might have stood trial for murder. But no one dared to bring charges against the Tanners because of their numbers. Step up to testify against one and another would kill you before the trial date. I doubt I'd have lived long enough to capture more than one or two.'

'How *did* you manage against seven men?'

'I had right and I hope the Good Lord on my side. I managed to take out three of them before they knew someone was on their trail. The others got nervous and ran. They didn't know I was only one man. They assumed it was a band of vigilantes. By the time I had their number down to the last two men, it didn't matter that they had figured out they were running from only me.'

'And you killed them both in a gunfight.'

'Yes,' he admitted.

'Did you feel a sense of accomplishment? Did it give you a satisfaction or relief from the heartache?'

'Mainly it has given me nightmares.' Again, he was honest. 'I don't think many ordinary people are cut out to kill other human beings. It so happens I'm good with a gun and the killers I ran down were either afraid, nervous or hurried their shots. They were used to attacking in numbers, ambushing unsuspecting farmers or ranchers. In a face-to-face gunfight I had the advantage.'

Suzanne was silent for a short time, as if thinking over everything he had said. When she lifted her eyes and looked at him, he knew she had made a decision.

'You offered to help me save the ranch. How do you propose doing it?'

'Mackenzie has been counting on your goodness and reluctance to fight back,' Dace told her. 'You showed him a different side when your men drove off the rustlers on this attempt. He knows he's in for a fight now.'

'I don't want a bloody war, Mr Kelly. I would hate to be responsible for

163

getting anyone killed.'

'You can't survive if you don't fight back,' Dace replied. 'If you try and use logic and compassion with an aggressive, merciless enemy, you will end up losing everything dear to you. Strength and force is all people like Mackenzie understand.'

Suzanne faltered before his words. 'I . . . I know what you are saying is true, but . . . '

'Let me handle Mackenzie for you. It's the reason your brother sent me here.'

'Yes, but you aren't a hired killer! You just told me as much.'

'Whether it's a man's country or his property and livelihood, we all have a right and obligation to defend what we hold dear. I believe I can help you.'

She didn't look convinced, but Suzanne reached out and took Dace's hand between her own. 'When he was alive, I trusted Eldon to always do the right thing,' she said. 'Dace Kelly, I am going to give you my trust as well.' She grimaced from her own promise. 'Please don't let me regret the decision.'

'I'll do the best I can,' he vowed.

With a final nod, Suzanne got to her feet, walked to the lamp, blew it out and left the bunkhouse.

Dace lay back down, but his brain was turning over ideas. Mackenzie was used to having free rein to do as he pleased. The turning back of his rustlers had been his first taste of opposition. Knowing Dace had joined the game was going to alter the man's strategy. To combat the tyrant's next move, Dace needed some ideas of his own. It would take a well-thought-out plan to go up against his money and power. He needed a way to cut down the odds, a means of . . . Dace sat up straight, struck by a sudden inspiration.

Of course! I've got a hole card no one knows about. If I play my hand right, I might just turn the tables on Grover Mackenzie!

9

Professor was chipper the next morning. He was mending nicely and seemed to have suffered no permanent damage. Dace spoke to him in private before preparing to leave the house.

'What will you do?' Suzanne asked, after he left his friend.

'I've got to make a trip to Denver before I can start my job here. It should take me a week or less, but it's necessary if we want to win this range war.'

'What will a trip to Denver accomplish?'

'I don't know just yet. It's an idea I have, but there are no guarantees. Trust me, it's for the best.'

'All right, Dace,' Suzanne said quietly.

Nathan, who was still at the table, about choked while sipping his second cup of coffee. 'Did I hear you right?' he asked, obviously unaware of Suzanne's decision the previous night. 'You're going to trust Kelly?'

'It's what you wanted, isn't it?'

'Yeah, but I didn't think you'd take my advice.'

Dace glanced over at the young man. 'I'd just as soon no one knows what I'm up to. It would be best to keep quiet about my involvement for the time being.'

'We won't say a word, Dace,' Nathan replied.

'If anyone asks, I'm still after the man who shot Professor and you haven't heard from me since.'

'You got it.'

'Have Guido keep a close watch on the herd until I return. When I get back, I'll have a better idea about the best way to proceed.'

'We'll do as you say, Dace,' Suzanne was the one to speak. 'Be careful and hurry back.'

Nathan waited until Dace left the

house before he spoke.

'OK, Sue, what's going on?'

She sighed. 'I thought it would be wise to allow Dace Kelly to handle the problem with Grover. That's all.'

Nathan wasn't convinced he had heard her right. He went into the next room to confront Professor.

'Why the trip to Denver?' he asked the injured man.

'A situation has arisen that supersedes the immediacy of the turmoil here in the valley,' Professor replied.

'Huh?' Nathan said. 'What kind of situation?'

'I fear Dace has prioritized my predicament before your own,' Professor explained. 'However, in an odd turn of events, Dace is very likely serving multiple purposes by going to Denver — for me, for you and Suzanne, and for the ranch.'

Suzanne frowned, having overheard the conversation. 'What on earth are you talking about, Professor? What's Dace going to do in Denver?'

'Patience, my friends,' he said with a smile. 'Alas, all three of us must await Dace's return. Only then will we know what, if anything, was accomplished on his mission.'

⋆   ⋆   ⋆

Dace discovered Mayor Ellis was a pompous sort, a man favoring expensive cigars, forever attired in fancy hat and suit and usually sporting a pretty girl on his arm. Once Dace had finished investigating the man, he made two important visits. When satisfied he was ready, he entered the saloon and handed a note to the bartender to pass on to the mayor. He then retired to his room to await the mayor's arrival.

Ellis did not disappoint him. Five minutes before the appointed time, there came a knock at his door. Dace met the man with gun in hand and cast a wary look down the hallway, before allowing him to enter.

'You Granger's partner?' Ellis asked.

'I am if you brought what you owe us,' Dace replied in an icy tone of voice. 'Otherwise, you'd best find a fast horse and get out of town.'

Mayor Ellis patted his vest pocket. 'I don't intend to leave town, Kelly. Where's Granger?'

Dace let him inside, closed the door all but a crack and then he moved around to stand in front of Ellis.

'Granger is lying on his back in a hospital bed,' Dace informed him. 'He neglected to tell me that Perkins was riding with a deadly killer named Dace Kelly. That crazy gunman liked to have killed us both.'

'But you got Perkins?'

Dace removed a ring from his pocket and passed it to the mayor. 'This mean anything to you?' he asked. 'Got some kind of scribbling etched inside, but it don't look like it's written in English.'

Ellis gave a contented nod. 'It was a gift from Perkins's father.'

'Well, Granger said I should show it to you as proof we done the job.'

'All right,' Ellis said, passing back the ring along with a piece of paper from his pocket. 'Tell Granger I never doubted him.'

'He said we could trust you.' Dace uttered a cynical laugh. 'I guess it's better being your friend than your wife or partner.'

'Granger told you about that?'

'Hey, I'm a top hand with a gun, Mayor. I don't come cheap and I don't kill someone without knowing the reason why. It makes no difference to me that you hired your partner killed and then did away with your wife. I'm good at my job and keep my mouth shut.'

'Too bad my first wife didn't have your ethics,' the mayor grumbled. 'It was her big mouth that got her killed and forced me to hire Granger to get rid of Perkins.'

'I've heard enough,' Dace said, whipping out his gun to cover the mayor. Before the stunned man could react, he spoke up loudly. 'How about you two?'

The door pushed open and Judge Roper and a deputy US marshal were standing in the hallway. The marshal also had his gun drawn. He entered the room and immediately searched the mayor, removing a small derringer from his coat pocket.

'You're under arrest for the murder of Cal Lawrence, the bartender and your wife,' the marshal stated, 'plus the attempted murder of Bernard Perkins.'

'Hold on! There's been a mistake!' the mayor cried. 'I'm being framed!'

The judge shook his head. 'A rope is too good for a craven murderer like you, Mayor Ellis. If it was still an accepted punishment, I would order you to be drawn and quartered!'

'Wait a minute!' the mayor whimpered. 'I can help you! What if I tell you the names of the men who killed Cal and the bartender — that woman bystander too!'

'What do you think, Judge?' the marshal wanted to know.

'Might earn yourself life in prison

rather than a noose around your neck,' Roper allowed. 'You would have to name the killers and then testify against them in court. If you do that, I would consider the lesser punishment when sentencing you.'

Dace stood back and listened. Once Ellis had told his story the marshal took him away. Judge Roper remained behind and looked at him.

'You did a real service here today, Kelly,' he allowed himself a grin, 'and you didn't even kill anyone.'

'I told you how it was with Granger.'

Roper bobbed his head. 'I believe you and I'll have his death affirmed as an act of self-defence.'

'Thanks.'

'What about this other trouble you've gotten yourself into?'

Dace explained the situation, starting from the time he and Professor had left Canyon City, ending with his idea for a solution. Roper pondered on the information for a short while before he commented.

'There's only one way to do this legally, so you don't end up in my court again. It's about as unorthodox as anything I've ever sanctioned, but the end would justify the means. Are you game?'

'I'll do my best not to kill anyone this time.'

Roper grunted. 'I should get that in writing . . . along with your deposition, which I'll need as evidence for the trial. With both the marshal and I being witnesses to the confession, Mayor Ellis won't have much he can use as a defence.'

'Justice at last for the daughter of the woman Ellis got killed,' Dace said. 'I think she'll be pleased with the news.'

'Let's go over to the courthouse so we can tend to our business. I'm sure you want to get back over the mountains as soon as you can.'

'You got it, Judge. I need to act before Mackenzie gets organized for another raid.'

10

Dace arrived at the ranch shortly after sundown. He approached the house carefully, in case someone was standing guard with a rifle. Before he could dismount a man appeared from the shadows justifying his precaution.

'You're back,' Guido spoke up, moving out where Dace could see him clearly. 'Mrs. Greer told me you had gone off for a few days.'

'Any trouble since I left?'

'Been quiet so far,' he replied. 'Professor returned to town yesterday. We took him by wagon so it wouldn't jar him as much as being on horseback. He was eager to get started on a story.'

'He'll like hearing the news I have then.'

Guido's teeth shown with a wide smile. 'I hear you caught up with the guy who bushwhacked Professor.'

'It ties in with the news I have for him. He'll be glad to know he doesn't have to look over his shoulder any more.'

'The boss lady said you promised to lend a hand in our trouble here.'

'I could use some help,' Dace told him. 'Are you and your cousins up for some payback?'

'Tell me what you need, Kelly.'

'Mind sharing the bunkhouse tonight?'

'I'll put up your horse and talk to you when you're ready to turn in for the night. We just finished eating, but I expect there are enough leftovers to take the edge off your appetite.'

'Thanks, Guido,' Dace said, 'I'll be along in a little while.'

The ranch foreman took the reins of Dace's horse and began to lead the animal toward the corral. Before Dace could approach the front door, it swung open wide and Nathan stood framed in the opening.

'Thought I heard voices out here,' he said. 'We've still got supper on the table, Kelly. Come on in.'

Dace enjoyed some light conversation while Suzanne put together a plate of leftovers. After making short work of the meal, Nathan went into the sitting-room while Dace used a towel to dry dishes while Suzanne washed. Once they had finished and the dishes were put away, Dace took a newspaper clipping out of his back pocket and handed it to her to read.

'What's this?' she asked, sitting down at the table.

'Something you should find of interest,' he said, taking a chair across from her.

Suzanne began to read the article and suddenly gasped. 'It can't be!' she cried. 'But how did you . . . ?'

'Most of the credit goes to Professor,' Dace explained. 'He began working on the story and spoke to the mayor's wife before he ended up in prison.'

'Yes, he told me about it.'

'I used the information and Granger's death to set a trap.'

'This report says Mayor Ellis is charged with murdering his wife, along with my mother and the other two men in the saloon.'

'Also the attempted murder of Professor,' Dace filled in the missing text. 'I believe the judge agreed to drop some of the charges for the mayor's future testimony against the men he hired to do the murders.'

Suzanne stopped reading and stared at him. 'You know who the three men are?'

'Better than that . . . I know *where* they are.'

It was a harsh look, as if eyeing some clumsy ox who had just ruined her best dress. The multiple expressions covered everything from stark realization to abhorrence. Her internal struggle took some time before she recovered her composure.

'You have a decision to make, Suzanne,' he said quietly. 'What do you want to do about those three men?'

The lady's eyes were watering with

tears and she lowered her head. 'You know what I want to say,' she murmured.

'You would like to see them dead,' he concluded.

'God forgive my desire for revenge, but yes, that's how I feel. I have wished for nothing more since the day those animals murdered my mother.' She seemed to swallow to stifle a sob. 'Is that so very wrong? Am I a sinner for such evil thoughts?'

'I can't believe you're asking *me* such a question.'

She blinked back her tears and regarded him with a steadfast scrutiny. 'Is it possible to get justice, Dace? Tell me the truth, will someone arrest those three killers and put them in jail? Will they hang from the gallows for their crimes?'

'Would that be enough to satisfy you?'

Without hesitation she answered 'Yes.'

He smiled at her resolve. 'You're a

better person than me, Suzanne. I didn't even try the lawful route.'

'Maybe not, but you didn't have anyone on your side. You told me how anyone who stood up against the Tanners ended up dead. I'm not in this alone' — she displayed a grim simper — 'I have Dace Kelly.'

'All right, it's settled,' he said. 'I'll personally see to it those men end up before Judge Roper. Whether they hang or go to prison will be up to him and a jury.'

'You're sure they are the men who killed my mother?'

'The one man is Sonny Leets, but his pals call him *Spider*.'

Suzanne sucked in her breath at hearing his name. 'One man called out for Spider to hurry up,' she recounted.

'And Ellis named them as the three men who did the killing.'

She reached across the table and took his hand in her own. 'I shouldn't have been so rude to you upon your arrival. I didn't give you a chance, wouldn't listen to a single word.'

'Far as you knew I was no different than the kind of gunman Mackenzie hired.'

'But you're not.'

'No, I won't steal or kill for money.'

'What if I had asked you to kill those three men?' she asked.

Dace chuckled. 'I didn't figure you would ask, but no, I would have tried to sway you to let justice work. With Ellis to testify against those killers, they should all end up dancing at the end of a rope.'

Suzanne smiled — she had a very attractive smile. 'I told you how I had been forced to be strong since my mother's death. It's a huge relief to have someone to share my problems with, someone I can trust to be truthful and sensible.'

'With luck, I aim to help you get a little more relief before I'm done,' Dace said. 'If everything goes as planned, you and Nathan might never have to worry about Mackenzie again. Your ranch could end up more prosperous than you had imagined.'

'What are you talking about?'

Dace grinned. 'You'll see when you read the first edition of the *Tolerance Post.*'

That caused her to arch her brows. 'The what?'

'Professor is going to put out a newspaper, or more aptly a newsletter . . . it will explain a lot.'

'How can he print any kind of newspaper? There's no printing press in town, he has no shop or office and he's not even fully recovered from being shot!'

'Trust me, Suzanne,' Dace said. 'I've got a plan. I'll need a little help from Guido and the boys, but it can work.' He rose to his feet to leave, but she held tightly to his hand.

Rising to her feet as well, Suzanne stepped over in front of him. She appeared to read his features, trying to deduct some hidden meaning in his eyes. 'I . . . I have never . . . ' She shook her head, as if searching for the right words. 'I-I feel as if . . . ' Her voice became a mere whisper, 'I think you are the man I've been looking for.'

Dace tried to circle his wagons, collect his thoughts, but he was caught totally unprepared.

'I can't describe the way I feel,' Suzanne murmured. 'It's . . . it's as if the weight of the world has been lifted off of my shoulders.'

'I'm going to ask Guido to stay close by, in case I need him and his cousins to help with my plan.' He lifted his hand before she could ask the question. 'I hope it won't be anything dangerous.'

'I'm sure Guido will agree to stay here at the ranch until this is over,' she said, moving a single step closer.

Dace wondered at the flush in her cheeks, the unusually rapid rise and fall of her chest, the way the golden flakes about her irises seemed to glow like a shower of sparks. His arms ached from the desire to hold her.

'There's a lot to do yet,' Dace warned

softly, recovering his power of speech. 'I've a hard job ahead, so I need to keep my wits about me. It wouldn't be wise for us to get too . . . personal until this is over.'

Suzanne nodded her head in agreement. 'I understand completely,' she murmured — then she kissed him.

★ ★ ★

Professor was up and had washed and shaved by the time Dace arrived. When he heard the news he was ecstatic.

'You bought me a printing press?' He was as gleeful as a child on Christmas morning. 'I can't believe it!'

'It's one of those small presses, the kind that only makes a single page at a time. It isn't an actual newspaper press.'

'Yes, but it's a grand start!'

'The freight wagon should be here about noon. I want you to start work on the things I've told you.'

'You can count on me, Dace. We'll rid this country of evil doers and

184

promote a new vitality and spirit of wholesome unity! We shall carve our own manifest destiny!'

Dace enjoyed his enthusiasm. 'In the meantime, Guido told me Mackenzie's ranch manager might be willing to negotiate a deal.'

'You will need leverage to coerce the man into double-crossing his boss.'

'I've a proposition he might find to his liking.'

Professor accepted his notion and turned to other matters. 'As you requested of me, before you left for Denver, I have spoken to a number of prominent people in Tolerance. Jason Dower and Bo Simpkins are our only two solid supporters. Others may follow if we demonstrate a degree of success.'

Dace approved with a nod. 'Don't release any news until I give you the word. We don't want Mackenzie to have time to muster a defence or fight back.'

'I shall await your given order, Dace. Where do you propose I set up the printing press?'

'When I was playing cards that first night in town, Dower mentioned he owned the empty shop next to his store. Ask him about leasing the place.'

'And what skulduggery — though I'm certain you will do nothing illegal — do you have planned?'

'I saw Mackenzie's horse at the livery. With him in town, it should give me a chance to speak to his ranch manager alone.'

'That would be Vince Kendall?'

'Yes, I'm hoping to head off a fight and maybe get a leg up on Mackenzie. Once he knows what's going on, he will have to fight back. The less odds against us at that time, the better our chance of success.'

'I wholeheartedly support that strategy, Dace. I wouldn't want the first edition of my newsletter to be the last.'

Dace returned Professor's ring and bid him farewell. He had to stop by Dower's store and send a telegraph message. With any luck, there might already be a message or two waiting for him. Next, he would pick up his horse and head for Mackenzie's ranch. It was time to stir the pot and, once the hot grease hit the fire, someone was going to get burned!

* * *

Vince Kendall was on the long side of thirty, with a Mexican wife and two kids. His greeting was reserved and there was a cool alertness in his eyes. He asked his wife to bring them each a glass of lemonade and offered Dace a chair on the front porch. Kendall's wife was there with drinks in hand before they had settled into their chairs.

'Much obliged, Mrs Kendall,' Dace said, offering her a smile.

'You don't bring us any trouble, *por favor*,' she replied softly.

'No, ma'am, I'm on a mission of peace.'

That loosened the tight little frown she had been sporting. 'Then welcome to our home.'

He thanked her again and took several swallows of the lemonade. It was tart, but not sour, and it was cold.

'Say, this hits the spot, Kendall. A cold drink is not something I would have expected out here.'

'We have an ice house out back. Last year we made it to the first freeze before we used up our store.' He puffed up his chest. 'Cut it right out of the lake ourselves and bring it down in blocks. Cold, miserable work, but it pays off during the summer months.'

Dace reached into his pocket and removed a piece of paper. He handed it to Kendall and waited for his reaction. It didn't take but a glance and the man sat upright.

'Whoa! Where the hell did you get this?'

'I'm looking for a man I can trust, Kendall.' Dace didn't answer the question, but reached out and took back the piece of paper. 'There's a passel of trouble coming and I want to avoid any unnecessary bloodshed or fighting.'

'Why come to me?'

'I've been told you're a cattleman at heart, not a gunfighter. I need to know you're honest and I can trust you.'

Kendall sat back and no longer made eye contact. 'You asked me that question, when you likely know something of our rather prolific herd?'

'Are you guilty of using a running iron to alter brands?'

He was stung by the bluntness of the question, but he locked gazes with Dace boldly. 'I was hired to run the ranch, Kelly. I don't condone what's been going on, but I need this house for my family. I look the other way concerning the mysterious appearance of extra cattle and do my job.'

'Who does the actual rebranding?'

'Three lowlife maggots Mackenzie keeps on the payroll, along with Top Perry and Joe Keyes, our foreman.'

'There's going to be a job here for a man to run this place, whether Mackenzie stays in charge or not. What I need is your word that you will not take up the fight against me or the Greer riders.'

'I've never been anything but a cattleman, Kelly,' Kendall said. 'It has taken me ten years to finally land a job where I have a real house for my family.'

'I'm not asking you to jeopardize your position or risk your family.'

'You take on Mackenzie, you're going up against a lot of fire power, Kelly. You might be the toughest critter to ever grab iron and throw lead, but a bullet in the back can kill you all the same.'

'All I want is your answer, Kendall. You don't really have a choice about the outcome, but I need your help to sort out the culls from the cowpunchers on this ranch.'

Kendall thought on it for a moment. 'Tell me what you expect of me and I'll give you my answer. Fair enough?'

Dace grinned. 'Fair enough.'

★　★　★

Chuck Lawry had been dozing, feet propped up on his desk, his head tipped down until his chin nearly rested on his chest. Dace shut the door to his office so it banged loudly and the man came awake with a start.

'Kelly?' he muttered. 'What the hell . . . ?'

'I'm going to need your jail cell, Sheriff,' Dace informed him. 'If you should decide to stay on as the town sheriff and guard the prisoners, I'll hold you personally responsible for their safekeeping.'

The man came to his feet, rubbing the sleep from his eyes and glowering at Dace.

'Come again?' He was wide awake but confused. 'You're asking me tuh do what?'

Dace placed three warrants on his desk. 'I picked these up in Denver — Golden actually, but they are legal and signed by a judge.'

Lawry picked up the notices and looked at the names. 'You're charging them boys with attempted rustling?'

'Read what it says at the top of the page, Sheriff. Those three men are wanted for murder.'

He was growing more confounded. 'Murder?'

'Maybe they were also in on the murder of Eldon Greer?'

Lawry snorted. 'Naw, I remember them fellas were right here in town the day he died.'

'So it was only you and Perry involved in the murder, huh?'

The words put an alarmed look on his face. 'I didn't have nuthing t' do with it a'tall! Top was the one who said there'd been an accident. If anyone kilt Greer it was him. I swear tuh yuh, Kelly, I've never broken the law in Tolerance, not since I pinned on this here badge.'

'You only sat by while your boss had his other hired men do the rustling and killing,' Dace remarked. 'Would that be what you call not breaking any laws?'

'You can't prove nuthin on me! I'm

192

the town peace keeper . . . that's it!'

'I wonder what a judge and jury will think.'

Lawry made a clumsy grab for his guns —

He stopped his draw at once . . . staring down the barrel of Dace's gun muzzle!

'Hot damn!' he mumbled in awe. 'You're quicker with your iron than any man I ever seen . . . and I've seen a few!'

'Back to the original subject, Sheriff. If you want to stay in Tolerance and wear the badge, I'm going to hold you responsible for the three men I lock up.'

'Where do yuh get off locking anyone up?' he wanted to know. 'Yuh start bounty hunting all of a sudden?'

'No,' Dace holstered his gun and pulled aside his vest to reveal a badge, 'I've been sworn in as a Deputy United States Marshal.'

Lawry stared at the badge and then looked Dace square in the eyes. 'I told you the truth, Kelly. I admit I've got my suspicions about some of the dirty deeds in the valley, but I've never soiled my hands or broken the law.'

'You never looked into Eldon Greer's murder or the cattle rustling from his spread either!'

'I'm a *town* sheriff,' Lawry whined. 'I don't have no jurisdiction beyond the city limits.'

'It's been your excuse up to this point, Sheriff, but it's time to ante up or get out of the game.' Dace gave him a hard look. 'When the shooting starts, I won't have time to think about all of your convenient excuses. I'm liable to put a bullet in you by mistake.'

'So what're my choices?'

'First option, keep the badge and do the job of town sheriff. When the time comes, you might have to testify against Topper as to what you *really* know concerning the murder of Eldon Greer. Also how you suspect Mackenzie for ordering his murder and the cattle rustling operation.'

'Damn, Kelly!' Lawry whined. 'I

could end up dead real sudden.'

'Second option, you sit in the cell while I do all of the leg work myself. Then you will be sentenced along with Mackenzie for every one of his crimes.'

'I'm innocent I tell yuh!'

'Make your choice,' Dace ordered.

The sheriff lowered his head in defeat. 'Don't suppose there's a third option?'

'You already tried that one,' Dace reminded him, 'when you drew against me.'

'Oh . . . right.'

'What'll it be, Sheriff? Either drop your gun and step into the jail cell, or give me your word you will guard the prisoners I put behind bars.'

'If I go along with your crazy plan, what then?'

Dace shrugged his shoulders. 'If you haven't lied to me about your involvement, you have nothing to fear from me.'

Lawry arched his brows in surprise. 'Yuh mean it?'

'The town will need a sheriff when this is over. Do the right thing and you might even keep the job.' Dace bore into him with an icy stare. 'Lie to me, or try a double-cross, and I'll follow you to the ends of the earth and shoot you dead.'

'Yuh can stop scaring me with your threats, Kelly,' the sheriff said quickly. 'I'll help yuh to arrest them thar varmits and sure 'nuff watch 'em fer yuh afterwards. I done give yuh my word.'

Dace's stare did not waver. 'I don't want you to talk to anyone from Mackenzie's place tonight and be ready to move first thing in the morning.'

11

It was fortunate that Smoker and Top Perry had gone out to the ranch the previous night. With roundup under way, even Grover was busy with overseeing his cattle. It left the three rustlers alone in town.

Dace took the sheriff, Bo and Dower to the saloon. They burst in upon the sleeping men and took them into custody without so much as a struggle. Within ten minutes the three men had been escorted to jail, where both the sheriff and Dower vowed to see they stayed behind bars.

Professor had been working all night and was pale from the exertion. He still offered Dace a smile when he entered the small office.

'One hundred copies!' he exclaimed. 'And I have hired two youngsters to deliver a page to everyone within a mile of town. By noon there won't be a soul in Tolerance who doesn't know what's going on.'

'I'll need a couple to take to the ranch.'

Professor forked over two sheets and Dace took a moment to scan the print. 'This is great stuff,' he praised Professor's work. 'It's exactly what I wanted.'

'I can't imagine you having the faintest inkling of a doubt,' Professor said. 'Have I not dazzled you with my ostentatious verbosity since the commencement of our camaraderie?'

'If that means you talk like a walking dictionary, yeah, I figured you were up to the chore.'

Professor laughed shortly but grew serious. 'I saw you and a couple men from town pass by with the three scoundrels responsible for the death of Suzanne's mother. I'm certain she will be pleased.'

'It's only the beginning.'

'I have found someone to take a copy of the newsletter to the Mackenzie

Ranch, as you requested. The custodian who cleans up at the saloon is going to ride out there this morning. Cost me my last two bits.'

'He knows to take the copy to Kendall?'

'As you instructed.'

Dace gave a nod of approval. 'Things are going to move quickly from this point on. I want you to close up shop and find a place to keep out of sight until the arrests have been made.'

'I am able to hold a gun,' Professor said with some spunk. 'If you need my help . . . '

'Keep a gun handy but stay out of sight. I don't want Mackenzie or one of his men trying to use you as a bargaining chip.'

'Ah, you mean a hostage situation, a possible prisoner exchange if I was captured.'

Dace shrugged. 'They are dumb enough to think I might actually trade for you.'

A look of alarm entered Professor's

face, but faded when Dace grinned to show he had been teasing.

'It's settled,' he said crisply, 'I shall be as hard to locate as a green-feathered chicken.'

Dace grinned. 'I seen one with a few green feathers once at a county fair . . . something called a bantam rooster.' With a second grin, 'You kind of remind me of him sometimes.'

'Obviously a noble fowl.'

Dace laughed. 'I'll see you later.'

Professor called to him as he left the shop, 'See that you have all your body parts intact!'

★ ★ ★

Guido was working at the corral as Dace approached the ranch house. By the time he arrived in the yard, the foreman had called to the house and Nathan and Suzanne joined him on the porch to greet him.

'Guido,' Dace wasted no time with small talk, 'I need you and the Lopez brothers to ride with me.'

The man didn't even glance back for Suzanne's approval. He trotted toward the corral and immediately caught up a horse.

'It will take him about thirty minutes,' Nathan told Dace.

'Yes, come in and have something to eat,' Suzanne suggested. 'I have some eggs, bacon and bread for toast.'

'Sounds good,' Dace replied, dismounting and tying off his horse.

'So what's been happening?' Nathan wanted to know. 'Wayde and three others from the Mackenzie ranch passed by here not an hour ago. Stopped long enough to tell us they were leaving the country and wouldn't be back. Didn't say why.'

Dace heaved a sigh of relief. 'Wayde was the foreman who oversaw the herd,' he explained. 'The man might not have rustled any of your cattle, but he sure enough knew where those beef came from. I'm betting Kendall warned him to get out of the valley. The men with him were probably those who helped him handle the stolen cattle.'

'But why run now?'

Dace went with them into the kitchen, removed the newsletters from his pocket and handed one to each of them. Nathan read the headline and whistled. Suzanne gasped and immediately sat down.

'Mackenzie bankrupt!' she exclaimed aloud. 'Wanted by the law for questioning with regard to murder and rustling!'

'And this item!' Nathan cried, pointing to a subheading. 'Three local men arrested for murder and robbery at a Golden, Colorado, saloon!'

'They are behind bars,' Dace told Suzanne. 'A prison wagon will be arriving in a day or two. Those three men are going to pay for killing your mother.'

She bolted up out of the chair. Dace barely had time to get to his feet before she threw her arms around him. Her tears were a mixture of happiness and pent-up grief. 'It's been so long,' she sobbed, 'so long in coming!'

'But how?' Nathan asked. 'I can't believe Chuck Lawry had the guts to arrest them by himself.'

'I arrested them,' Dace told him. 'I was deputized before I left Golden.'

Suzanne pushed away and stared at him in wonder. 'A man right out of the state prison? He deputized you?'

'He's the one who sent me to prison,' Dace clarified. 'He's also one of the men who vouched for me so I could get out early.' Dace took a moment to explain how they had trapped Ellis into a confession and why he was sent back with a badge. He finished with, 'Roper wants it legal this time.'

'But Mackenzie has so many men,' Suzanne worried. 'How can you go up against them all by yourself?'

'Dower and Bo, from the livery, helped us arrest the three rustlers for murder. Wayde and some of the others have already made a run for parts unknown. When I ride out to Mackenzie's ranch, I'll have Kendall and most of the regular cowboys on my side.'

'It still sounds dangerous.'

'Is that why you need our crew?' Nathan asked.

'Yes, they shouldn't have to do anything more than herd a few head of cattle.'

Suzanne sighed. 'It all sounds so unbelievable.'

'A brand inspector for the state is due to arrive this morning. We will ride out to the Mackenzie ranch and cut out every cow with an altered brand and return them to you.'

'Hot damn!' Nathan shouted . . . immediately cowed by a stern look of disapproval for his language from Suzanne. He quickly suppressed his elation. 'Uh, I mean, this is great news!'

The young lady moved over to the stove, once again a perfect hostess. She prepared breakfast and set down the plate for Dace. All the while he ate, they discussed the situation. Both were hopeful for the return of fifty or so head of cattle. It would be enough to help pay the mortgage payment and allow them to make payroll for their hired hands.

Guido arrived moments after Dace had finished eating. The three Lopez brothers were with him, all packing rope and rifles, ready for whatever lay ahead. Nathan limped out to the porch so he could wish them luck.

'I can't delay,' Dace told Suzanne. 'I've got to move before Mackenzie can get organized. I wouldn't want him trying to free the three prisoners or muster up any extra firepower. Once he reads the newsletter, the bull is going to be out of the pen.'

'Before you leave,' Suzanne whispered, so Nathan would not hear, 'I . . . I wanted to be clear about' — she blushed noticeably — 'about . . . well, you know.'

'Took me a little by surprise,' Dace said.

'Yes, well, I didn't mean to . . . that is, it wasn't my intention to . . . to . . . '

Dace moved to within inches of her.

'Letting you kiss me was my own fault,' he said quietly.

She regarded him with a puzzled look. 'Your fault?'

He took hold of her shoulders and gently coerced her into his arms. 'Yes,' he admitted. 'I should have been the one making the advances.' And he rectified the mistake by kissing her firmly on the mouth.

* * *

Kendall was on the porch by the time Dace, the brand inspector and the Lopez boys rode up to the house.

'Mackenzie was here when the newsletter arrived,' Kendall said right off. 'He did a lot of swearing and left to find Smoker, Keyes and Topper.'

'Makes sense,' Dace replied. 'They will be the men I put behind bars.'

'I have the record books here,' Kendall offered. 'This the brand inspector with you?'

'Bill Hanes,' the inspector introduced

himself. 'I personally watched them arrest the man responsible for allowing Mackenzie's altered brands to be sold for market. Do you have an accounting record of your own?'

Kendall stepped over and handed him a sheet of paper. 'This is the number of cattle we own and have sold officially. You can compare it with your sales receipts and we should know exactly how many cattle were stolen from the Greer ranch.'

Bill looked over the totals. 'Looks like there's a considerable difference.'

'We intend to make it right,' Dace told him. 'If it takes every steer on the place, we have to balance the scales.'

'The herd is gathered at the base of the east pasture,' Kendall advised them. 'I've given orders for every one of our men to be there. You'll have all the help and co-operation you need.'

Dace turned to Guido. 'You and your cousins go with Bill and handle the cattle,' he told the man. 'I need to locate Mackenzie before he gets away.'

Guido shook his head. 'Luis and his brothers can handle the cattle. I'm riding with you.'

'I have help in town,' Dace said.

'Yes, an old man from the livery and a storekeeper. Not the kind of help you can count on in a gunfight.'

'I'm hoping there won't be a gunfight.'

'Me, too, but I'm tagging along all the same.'

They parted company with the others and started for town. They hadn't gone far before they met up with two men, standing in the road blocking the trail. The man Dace didn't recognize had his gun trained on Smoker!

'Light down, Kelly,' he greeted them. 'My name is Randal Keyes and I have a proposition for you.'

Dace handed the reins of his horse to Guido and dismounted. He moved to within thirty feet and waited to see what the two men were up to.

'Ever since you arrived in this valley,' Keyes began, 'me and the others have listened to Smoker here brag about how he should have killed you the first night you arrived at the Greer ranch. We have all grown sick from listening to his bragging and big-man talk.'

'So what's the deal, Keyes?' Dace asked. 'Why the gun?'

'I'm getting to it,' the man replied. 'You see, Smoker is Mac's top gun, his big dog. I've always been second, kind of like a fifth wagon wheel.' He grinned. 'We all know what dogs do to wagon wheels.'

Dace could have commented or drawn his gun to cover Keyes, but he held his silence and waited to see what the man had up his sleeve.

'When the time came to kill old man Miller, Smoker was the man who done it. He bragged about how the old boy had tried to draw against him — real challenge, seeing how Miller carried an old Navy Colt he probably hadn't fired since he bought it. Anyway, every chore that needed doing, Smoker was the man for the job.' Keyes chuckled. 'Even when it came time to follow you around, it was Smoker who got the order.' His smile faded. 'And after you caught him watching you, he again told us how, if only Mac would turn him loose, he could have killed you on the spot.'

'I guess I owe Mackenzie for allowing me to live this long,' Dace said drily. 'What is your proposition, Keyes?'

'I want to see how fast Smoker . . . and you really are,' Keyes said pointedly. 'I'm out of it, because I ain't got no reason to run from you. I've been on the job for over a year and never done one blessed thing outside the law.'

'All right,' Dace told him, 'so you haven't committed any crimes. Now what?'

'Empty that snake killer on your hip of all but one bullet,' Keyes told him, swinging the gun to cover him. 'I've already done the same with Smoker's gun.'

'I don't know what your — '

'Do it!' Keyes commanded, keeping the pistol trained on Dace. 'And then step over here next to Smoker.'

Dace emptied his pistol except for one round. Smoker glowered at Keyes as Dace warily slipped his gun back into its holster.

'This is real simple contest,' Keyes explained, tipping his head to indicate a direction. 'There are two empty gallon cans fifty feet off the trail. Kelly, you take the one on the right and Smoker can take the one on the left.'

'I got no reason to play your silly game,' Smoker growled at Keyes. 'When I shoot the can my gun is empty and Kelly can arrest me.'

'That's the sporting part of this here game,' Keyes replied. 'If you are the fastest to hit the can, I'll keep Kelly right here and let you ride away — fifteen minutes' head start ought to be fair.' He grinned. 'Of course, all you'll really need is time to reload because Kelly will know you can beat him in a gunfight.'

'And if Kelly should win?'

'You're his prisoner,' Keyes stated. 'Can't make the game any simpler than that.'

Dace hid the smile that threatened to come to his face. Keyes had put up with Smoker's bragging until he'd had enough. He had thought up this as a way to get even.

Yeah, cute idea . . . but only if I win!

'On my count,' Keyes said, moving around behind the two of them, 'and no fudging or doing something stupid, like trying to shoot me or each other. You both draw and fire at your target on *three*.'

Dace felt rather silly, facing an empty paint can, but he dismissed the sensation. Smoker had killed the rancher named Miller and his name was on several wanted posters. If not for Keyes, Smoker could have ambushed him and Guido or made good his escape.

Keyes began the count precisely, no hesitation, no quick count. 'One . . . two . . . three!'

Dace's gun didn't flash to his hand, it materialized as if from thin air. He squeezed off the round with the ease which came from years of practice. His can was spilling over as Smoker fired his own pistol . . . and missed! It hadn't even been close.

Keyes let out a holler and gleefully holstered his gun. 'Tell me about your prowess with a gun now, Smoker!' he taunted the mortified gunman.

'Shooting a can ain't the same as facing a man,' Smoker muttered a lame response.

'You're right about that,' Keyes told him. 'If I had let you try besting Kelly in a gunfight, you'd be sitting down to a hot meal with the Devil right now without knowing you'd died and gone to Hell!'

'What now?' Dace asked him.

Keyes looked over. 'That's it,' he said. 'Smoker is all yours and I'm riding out and not looking back.'

'I'll wish you luck, so long as you stay on the right side of the law,' Dace told him. 'Any idea where Mackenzie is?'

After mounting his horse, Keyes gave Dace a serious look. 'He and Topper headed for town. He was going to try and pick up his three men from the jail and then do some damage to the Greer place as he left the valley. You're maybe ten minutes behind him.'

There wasn't time to thank Keyes. The man spun about and put heels to his horse's ribs. Guido covered Smoker until Dace and the gunman were both mounted. There was a new sense of urgency to reach the jail. He needed to get to the Greer ranch!

12

Suzanne saw the approaching pair of riders and her heart sank. It was not Dace and Guido, but Grover and Top Perry.

'Nate!' she called to her stepbrother. 'Get out the back way and hide!'

'I can't leave you here,' he shot back.

'They won't hurt me; Grover isn't that stupid.'

Nathan took the rifle and hurried as fast as his crippled body would let him, disappearing out the back door of the house. To cover his movements Suzanne walked boldly out the front door and waited for the two horsemen to stop in the yard.

'Have you had a chance to read the newsletter Bernard Perkins put out today?' Her tone was derisive. 'It reads that you are broke!'

Grover's face was dark with fury and

he bared his teeth in a sneer. 'Your brother managed this double-cross! He sent Kelly here to bankrupt me!'

'No, Bill sent Kelly here to stop you from bankrupting me.'

'You think you've won.' He snorted. 'Well, think again, you haughty little prude! Kelly may have saved your place, but that doesn't mean he can save you!'

'You touch me and every lawman for a thousand miles around will be looking for you,' she warned.

'Where's your gimpy kid brother, or son, or whatever the hell he is?'

'Nathan is watching the cattle. All of my riders went to retrieve my stolen cattle from your ranch.'

'You think you're going to get the last laugh do you?' Grover growled the words, 'Well, think again, sweetheart!' He tipped his head as a signal to Top.

The man swung down from his horse and grabbed hold of Suzanne's arms. He began to drag her toward the house.

'Make sure she doesn't get out!'

Grover called to him. 'It has to look like an accidental fire.'

Before Top could reach the door with the struggling woman, Nathan appeared at the side of the house. He had the rifle level and aimed at the big man.

'Turn her loose or die!' he cried.

Top let go, only to make a grab for his gun. Grover drew his pistol at the same time. Nathan panicked and pulled the trigger. Top took the slug to the middle of his chest and toppled over on to his back.

Grover fired at Nathan and the boy cried out in shock. He was knocked off of his feet and the rifle flew from his hands. Grover swiveled in the saddle to fire at Suzanne, but he heard the pounding hoofs of a rider coming hard.

Dace was too far away for an accurate shot, but he fired high to get Mackenzie's attention. It was a clean miss but the man turned his gun toward him and returned fire, missing three times. However, the fourth round hit Dace hard in the left arm and he lost the reins to his charging horse. He kept his gun trained, knowing he had to stop Mackenzie before he tried again to kill Suzanne. Even as Grover took a more careful aim, Dace got off a good shot of his own.

Mackenzie was rocked back in the saddle and fell from his horse. He landed on his side, but rolled over and got back up to his feet. Dace's horse continued to close the distance. He sought a clear shot, but Mackenzie's mount danced around and got in the way. The spooked animal also caused Mackenzie to miss his next shot.

The horse suddenly bolted — Dace prayed for a steady hand and fired again.

Mackenzie grunted from the bullet, hit hard this time. Instead of trying to get off another shot at Dace, the mortally wounded man sought his revenge against Suzanne.

Lacking guidance from the reins, the horse turned —

Dace shouted 'Whoa!' at his horse

and the animal slid to a jarring, uneven halt. Dace fought to remain in the saddle and twisted about, desperately seeking to bring his gun to bear.

But Mackenzie was already pulling the trigger, his gun aimed directly at Suzanne!

Because of his numb left arm and still holding his pistol in his right hand, Dace half fell and half dismounted, landing on his knees. He clung to the pistol and took aim.

Dace didn't have to shoot. Mackenzie had already pulled the trigger . . . several times, but he had run out of bullets.

'Damn you, Suzanne Greer!' Mackenzie swore vehemently. 'I could have had it all. I could have been king of the valley.'

Suzanne didn't pay him any mind, hurrying over to check on Nathan. Dace got to his feet, walked up to the man and poked him in the chest with his gun. 'Why don't you do everyone a favour and drop dead!'

Mackenzie was swaying uncertainly, his life's blood soaking his fancy vest. 'I ain't doing you no favors, Kelly,' he muttered hoarsely. 'I'll die when I'm good and ready.'

Dace saw Nathan was on his feet and felt a wave of relief. 'Maybe you ought to stick around for your murder trial, Mackenzie. That's a hanging I'd like to see.'

But the man folded at the knees and fell forward onto his face. It took only a glance to see he was not sticking around for anything.

'Hit the stock of the rifle!' Nathan was explaining to Suzanne. 'I thought I'd been hit, but it was the force of the bullet batting the gun against my chest that knocked me down.'

'Good thing you were able to stop Topper,' Dace told the boy. 'I couldn't get here any quicker.'

'You're injured!' Suzanne cried, hurrying over to look at his wound.

Dace gingerly moved the left arm. 'Bullet must have nicked the bone,' he said. 'It was numb for a few seconds, but I'm getting feeling back now.'

'Get your shirt off and let me take a look at it.'

Dace shrugged out of his shirt and discovered an angry tear alongside his bicep, but it had stopped bleeding. 'A simple bandage is about all I need,' he said.

'What happened to the rest of Grover's men?' Suzanne asked.

'Smoker is in jail. Mackenzie didn't try to break out his men once he saw three men were guarding them.'

'And the cattle?'

'Your men, along with a couple of mine, are driving back about two hundred head.'

Suzanne gasped. 'Two hundred head!'

'Kendall had the records of the number sold legally. The brand inspector was able to match the sales records from the last two years.'

'Wait a minute!' she said, frowning. 'What did you mean — a couple of your men are coming with our riders?'

Dace turned his shirt in his hands so he could remove a piece of paper from his pocket. 'Oh, did I forget to tell you? I now own the Mackenzie ranch. I picked up his deed in Denver, and without the extra cattle, he can't pay the mortgage payment. Seems he was already six months in arrears so I foreclosed on his place.'

'You did what?' she was dumbfounded. 'But where did you get the money?'

'From your old pal Mayor Ellis. He paid me five thousand dollars for killing Professor.'

Suzanne was stunned by the news, but shielded her eyes to look down the trail toward town. 'Looks as if Professor and Guido are coming.' Then with a glance at the two dead men, 'They are a little late to do much here.'

'Professor can put our engagement in his next newsletter,' Dace suggested.

'He can do what?' she cried.

Dace smiled. 'Just think of it, Suzanne, once we're married, we'll have one of the biggest spreads in Colorado. Nathan can manage the payroll and bills, while Kendall oversees the cattle, bookkeeping and expenses.'

'Hey! That's great!' Nathan said, smiling at them both. 'You two are getting married?'

'I . . . I haven't said I would marry you, Dace Kelly,' Suzanne sputtered, her cheeks crimson with embarrassment. 'We don't know each other all that well.'

'Once I get those prisoners back to Golden for their trials, we'll have plenty of time for courting.'

'Well,' she recovered quickly, displaying a coy simper, 'as long as you put it that way.'

'Hot dang!' Nathan cried. 'I'm gonna have me a new brother-in-law . . . or is it a stepfather?'

'We can work it out when the time comes . . . partner.'

Nathan beamed. 'Yeah, *partner* sounds good to me.'

Suzanne laughed. 'Yes, me too.'

Professor and Guido pulled up in time to hear the final exchange.

'Did I hear correctly,' Professor wanted to know, 'you three are partners?'

'Four,' Dace corrected. 'You are the one who helped us catch the men responsible for the murder of Suzanne's mother. It was your being shot that led to the arrest of Mayor Ellis for his wife and business partner. And the money paid for your pretended death is how I was able to assume control of Mackenzie's place.'

'I have no desire to tend cattle or dwell on a ranch for all my days,' Professor replied. 'The printing press you bought me will suffice as payment. Once I sell this story back East I shall be famous.' He paused to smile at the three of them. 'Obviously, I will need a happy ending.'

Dace put his good arm around Suzanne and rested his left hand on Nathan's shoulder. 'We will certainly try to manage that much for you, Professor. We certainly will!'

Other titles in the
Linford Western Library:

LIGHTNING AT THE HANGING TREE

Mark Falcon

Mike Clancey was the name inside the rider's watch, but many people during his travels called him Lightning. He was too late to stop a hanging, the men were far away when he reached the lonely swinging figure of a middle-aged man. Then a youth rode up and Lightning found out that the hanged man was his father. So why had he been hanged? Soon the two were to ride together in a pitiless search for the killers.